London Tales

a collection of short stories

By Tim Walker

London Tales

Text copyright © 2023 Timothy N. Walker
All rights reserved

No part of this publication may be reproduced, stored or transmitted in any form or by any means, electronic, mechanical, photocopying, recording, scanning or otherwise without written permission from the author.
It is illegal to copy this book, post it to a website, or distribute it by any other means without permission of the rights holder.
This collection of short stories is a work of fiction. Some details of the lives of historical figures are invented by the author, and some characters are fictitious. Historical settings and references to events are drawn from historical research sources that the author believes to be verified history, or surmised in the case of ancient history.
Any resemblance to actual persons, living or dead, or events is otherwise coincidental, excepting historical subjects named in the Author's Note.
Timothy Neil Walker asserts the moral rights to be identified as the author of this work.

Acknowledgements

The author wishes to thank the following for their invaluable help:
Friends and family for their critical feedback
Copyeditor – Amy Coombes (Gemini Editing)
Cover art & design – Sean McClean (via Upwork)

Independently published by

www.timwalker1666.wixsite.com/website

Contents

	Page
Introduction	4
Prologue	6
Londinium Falling	9
A Summer's Disquiet	30
Burning Shadows	48
Holly's Dream	68
Cherry Blossoms Fall	78
Brian's Beat	101
Part One – When We Were Young	101
Part Two – Let It Be	107
Part Three – The Stakeout	111
Part Four – The Waters of Time	115
Part Five – Nelson's End	117
Mac the Ripper	120
The Seesaw Sea of Fate	130
Geraniums	141
Blue Sky Thinking	153
Valentine's Day	159
Author's Note	190
About the Author	201

Introduction

This collection of eleven tales offers dramatic pinpricks in the rich tapestry of London's timeline, a city with two thousand years of history. They are glimpses of imagined lives at key moments, starting with a prologue in verse from the point of view of a native Briton tribeswoman absorbing the shock of Roman invasion. Then there's a tale set in Roman Londinium in 60 CE, from the perspective of terrified legionaries and townsfolk facing the vengeful Iceni queen, Boudica, whose army burnt the fledgling city to the ground.

From these glimpses of Roman Londinium there's a jump forward to the medieval city in 1381 at the time of the Peasant's Revolt, then a leap to the second significant conflagration, the Great Fire of London, in 1666. From there the reader is transported to 1814 and the last ice fair on the frozen Thames in the year before the battle of Waterloo. This is followed by a kitchen sink drama set during the Blitz in 1941; then the swinging Sixties and wide-flared seventies are remembered in the life story of fictional policeman, Brian Smith. Then follows an unnerving tale of copycat killings based on the 1888 Jack the Ripper murders.

There's a series of contemporary stories that reference recent history and current affairs, including the London terrorist bombings of 2005, a literary pub crawl and a daring prison break, building to the imagined death throes of London in a dystopian vision. These stories are loosely inspired by the author's personal experiences and reflections on his time living and working in London in the 1980's and 90's. Adaptability, resilience, conformity and resolve are recurring themes in these stories.

London is a remarkable city and rightly one of the world's best-known and most iconic. Waves of settlers from Continental Europe, the British Isles and Ireland have filtered in over hundreds of years, some seeking peace from conflict, to mix in with Londoners and forge a diverse and progressive society. Historically, new arrivals from Europe alighted from boats at the eastern docks and tended to funnel into the East End, often living in cramped and squalid conditions that are barely a mile from opulent townhouses and mansions in the wealthy West End. These two areas bookend the City of London, where the Bank of England sits on Threadneedle Street and glass towers rub shoulders with graceful historic buildings.

For ten years the author was one of thousands of commuters who'd pour in daily from outlying suburbs to feed the insatiable economic appetite of the city. London's a busy and at times unfriendly place, driven by the productivity of its inhabitants and set against an incredible landscape of history, art, architectural and cultural development. It both inspires and tires in equal measure.

Early versions of some of these stories appeared in the author's 2017 collection, *Postcards from London,* now unpublished. Those retained have been extensively revised and supplemented by a clutch of new stories. *London Tales* is a companion volume to *Thames Valley Tales.*

Tim Walker October 2023

Prologue

The Day Our World Changed

I am Arwen of the Catuvelauni people, once beloved of Rai, god of light
We were blessed with long days under Rai's season of plenty
When our barley sprouted life-giving buds and our animals fattened
We are fishers of the great river and hunters of the forest since time began.

But now we cry and spit the bitter taste of defeat
Our men slaughtered and our children weep
Only the young remain to harvest the crop
And us old ones must hull the barley till we drop.

Our gods fled when the soldiers of Rome found us
Their gods are more powerful and chased Rai from the sky
Our warriors fell before their ochre-stained shields
And the wings of their golden eagle cast a shadow across the land.

A chill wind blew along the track to our village that day
It swirled round the dead owl post that wards off evil spirits
And we ran to hide under cover of dark shadows
Listening from the forest to the rhythmic tramp of boots.

Clutching charms to protect us from evil and mumbling the words
Soon drowned by the jangle of metal and cries in a foreign tongue
Rai did not strike them as they entered our stockade of sharpened stakes
That keep out the animals of the forest and deter other tribes
But not the men from Rome, wherever that may be
In that moment we knew our gods had abandoned us.

They scattered the fowl, pigs and yapping dogs who cowered and whimpered
Their Trinovante guide told our chief they will pave our road to make it strong
What is a road? Our grey-haired elder asked
The narrow tracks that connect our villages have been there since the world began Given to us by our mother, Brigantia, who whispers in the wind
But our conquerors will make use of them to keep us at heel
They will put flattened rocks on stony pathways to connect their camps
They are here to stay.

Time passes and we have become accustomed to the men of Rome
They ask for our cooperation from behind a row of shields
The sunlight glistening off bosses, helmets and spear tips
Our new masters send men to show us how to grow their crops
Wheat, fruit and vegetables we have not seen before
They take our goats and fowl but give us only round bronze discs
This is their money, our elder says, to barter with at market.

Then they take our sons and mother's weep
Tears stain the cracked but unyielding earth
Our cries the anguish of the conquered
Powerless before the ever-watchful eagle of Rome.

Our druid tells us not to be afraid
But he runs to hide in the forest whenever they approach
Our sons come to visit and stand proud and tall
Dressed in the Roman fashion in togas and sandals of leather
We laugh and hug them and covet their shoes.

They have been taught Roman ways and can read their symbols
And now show their little brothers how to catch fish in nets
Laughter entwines with the splash and flash of silver as they take turns to cast it

London Tales

*Small stones drag the net to the depths where Father Tamesis
waits for an offering.*

*Our mighty River Tamesis flows since the dawn of men
It feeds and refreshes us and receives our sacrifices
And never lies nor betrays, but sometimes takes one of us
In the rushing flow that carries our hopes to the sea of life.*

*We are the new slaves of Rome but one day will be free
We place offerings to their gods in their temples of marble
But still meet in the oak groves where our druids chant
The Romans command us but they will never own our souls.*

*I am Arwen of the Catuvelauni people, once beloved of Rai,
god of light
We are blessed with long days under Sol and Rai's season of
plenty
When our wheat and barley spout life-giving buds and our
cattle fattens
We are fishers of the great river and hunters of the forest since
time began.*

*Once we cried and spat the bitter taste of defeat
When our men were slaughtered and our women wept
But our children grow strong as they harvest the crops
And us old 'uns give wise council 'til we shall drop.*

Londinium Falling

I

"Oi, you're cheating me! This die is weighted!" Marcellus threw the offending cube at the grinning, gap-toothed Lupus, who scooped both dice up and dropped them into a leather pouch, cackling like a hag.

"Pay up, Marcellus. It was a fair game," he crooned. The other legionaries laughed and slapped the luckless Marcellus on the back before walking away.

"It wasn't a fair game," Marcellus protested. "Show me those dice again." Marcellus could now see, playing the game back in his mind, that the number six hardly ever came up on the die he was given, whereas it seemed to always land on a six for his grinning opponent. Perhaps he switched to another die when it was his turn? "You've tricked me with weighted dice. I'm not paying you anything!"

Lupus's grin quickly turned to a scowl and his grey eyes narrowed with malice. "You will pay up, soldier, or you'll have to answer to my partner."

Brutus stood and cracked his knuckles, towering over the luckless legionary. Marcellus looked around into the darkness beyond the flickering light of the campfire and saw that he was alone. Brutus was the cohort wrestling champion and his favourite pastime was hurting people. Allied to the sly Lupus, they made a formidable team that had emptied the purses of many unsuspecting soldiers.

Marcellus eyed the monster with dread. He had lost most of his month's pay and realised, too late, that he would be unable to settle his rent arrears for the small two-room quarters he shared with his wife, Julia, and their six-year-old son, Cato, in a narrow street behind the main barracks in

Londinium. He rolled his two remaining denarii around in the palm of hand, wondering how far he would get if he ran.

Brutus, anticipating his flight, stepped forward and grabbed his woollen tunic in both hands, effortlessly lifting the smaller man who left a trail of dust falling from his sandals. He snarled as he locked eyes on the tanned Thracian, deciding what to do to him. He was interrupted from whatever he had in mind by a commotion that had sprung up around them as shouting legionaries ran past. Their unit optio, a seasoned veteran called Darius, appeared.

"Oi! Put him down and stand to." Brutus dropped Marcellus and all three legionaries stood to attention.

"What's happened, sir?" the grovelling Lupus asked.

Darius stood with his feet apart and his hand on the hilt of his gladius. "To add to the bitter news that our comrades at Camulodunum have been slain and the town burnt to the ground, it now seems that the witch-queen Boudica has chosen to visit us rather than Verulamium, and they're on their way. Get your armour on and report to your unit commander. Move!"

Lupus grabbed Marcellus as he attempted to run after Darius. "You will pay me, Marcellus, or Brutus will arrange for an unfortunate accident to befall you and your lovely wife," he hissed.

Marcellus pulled away and ran from the north gatehouse where they had been on night picket, past standing oil lamps on street corners, stumbling on uneven bricks as he dashed through the narrow, pre-dawn streets now alive with rushing soldiers and civilians, straight to his small, terraced house. Inside, he found his servant Androgeus helping Julia to pack their few valuable possessions into canvas backpacks. He scooped up his young son and planted a kiss on Julia's forehead.

"The garrison has been ordered to stand to. It looks like the rebel army will descend on us after all. Androgeus will take you to the dockside to await evacuation by galley." Androgeus was no slave, but a paid worker and a subject of Rome from the local Trinovante tribe, who claimed to be a descendent of King Lud, after whom the settlement was named. Though he was elderly and bent with hunched shoulders, he was still strong enough to pull a cart and lift heavy loads. He insisted on referring to his town as Ludinum.

Julia gasped at this unexpected and terrifying news. Marcellus smiled and looked into her eyes, now welling up with tears. "It won't come to that, my love. They may go elsewhere. But if they come, we'll hold them off, and evacuation is only a last resort. Now make ready. Carry some dried fruits and bread, and gourds of water. I have only these two denarii remaining, intended for rent, but you must take them." He forced the coins into her hand and closed her fingers around them. Marcellus quickly dressed for battle and tied on his calf-length leather sandals. His shield, body armour, gladius short sword and dagger were stored on his rack back at the barracks.

"Androgeus, lead them to the port by the safest route. I must go," he said, kissing his wife and child before putting on his plumed helmet and edging out of the door. "Make an offering to Fortuna for our safety at the temple on your way!" he shouted as he merged into the hubbub outside.

II

Marcellus had joined his unit on the northern perimeter, little more than a raised wooden platform behind an earth bank, looking out over a desolate marsh with only a few random, wooden shacks dotting the otherwise empty landscape. A heron took to the air with a shrill and lonely cry. He turned to his friend Septimus and said, "That lying, cheating weasel of a Gaul has cleaned me out with his weighted dice. I've given the last coins in my purse to my wife and sent her and the boy to the docks."

"You have an unhealthy liking for wine and dice, my friend," the Spaniard replied. "But none of that matters now. Money will not help us, only strong arms and sound tactics. We cannot throw coins portraying our divine emperors' heads at the Iceni."

From their wooden platform they looked down into a dry ditch, dug out the year before by slaves, and already becoming a dumping ground for human waste. In the centre of the bank was a wooden gatehouse and, at intervals of fifty paces, there were square, wooden towers that offered a platform for catapults and javelin throwers. The earth bank ran at right angles down to the river Tamesis, forming a rectangular space, bounded on the south side by the river.

Marcellus looked to his left over the tiled roofs of houses at an old stone monument that formed one side of the west gatehouse, called Ludgate by the locals. According to Androgeus, it was the burial site of old King Lud and his sons, one of whom was his grandfather whose name he bore. Marcellus grunted and spat to ward off the evil spirits of the dead, and wondered if his family was safe with the Briton.

The corner plot was marked out as a fort that could house a thousand men, most under leather tents, but now was garrisoned by just two cents of the Ninth Legion, comprising a little under two hundred regular soldiers, or legionaries, plus a handful of engineers and junior officers. In addition, there was an unruly cavalry unit of fifty Germanic auxiliaries whose main role was to patrol the hinterland. It was they that now came riding back at a gallop to report to the watch commander.

"Judging by their agitation and arm waving, I'd say the rebel army is fast approaching," Marcellus muttered to his mates. He took a swig from a flask of brandy passed along the line.

Since Londinium had been established on the ruins of King Lud's fortress by the army of Emperor Claudius just seventeen years previously, close to a thousand civilians were also crammed into the busy settlement - citizens, family members, traders, sailors, subjects, and slaves. It was a densely packed space, occupying close to a square mile, and some had moved to a growing settlement on the south bank of the river following the construction of a wooden bridge. Londinium was becoming an important staging post for moving legionaries and supplies north and westwards as the task of subduing the stubborn island continued.

In the centre of each of the three banks stood gatehouses that contained mighty hinged doors that were braced with thick, iron-cored beams. Tracks used by locals ran from the modest east and west gates, but the main paved road ran directly from the biggest gatehouse in the centre of the north bank. Beyond the marsh, the road forked, with the left road leading a day's march to a staging fort at Verulamium and the right leading to the capital of the Province of Britannia, Camulodunum. It was to the east that all eyes now looked as sprigs of smoke could be seen in the early dawn light.

Their unit commander, Optio Darius, appeared by their side, narrowing his eyes as he searched the horizon. "Keep your eyes peeled, men. Shout if you see anything."

"Aye sir," Marcellus replied, adding, "what is known of the cause of this rebellion? I thought the Iceni were our allies?"

Darius glared at him, taking a moment to decide whether to rebuke his impudence or give an answer. After a brief pause, he said, "Their king died, leaving half his lands in tribute to our divine emperor, Nero. So, Procurator Decianus decided to seize the remaining half to make farms for retired legionaries. I've heard that the dead king's widow, Boudica, was publicly flogged when she objected, and her daughters raped. Now she leads their vengeful army."

Marcellus sucked his teeth. "That's *serious* provocation."

"Indeed; and unwise given that our governor and commander, General Paulinus, has taken most of our garrison to the north to join with the Ninth Legion. And I'm sure you've noticed many of the wealthier townsfolk have also left to follow them, giving our town a feeling of partial abandonment." Darius's knuckles glowed white on the pommel of his gladius.

"This dung heap is clearly not worth defending," Marcellus muttered to the legionary next to him.

"Aye, and we are expendable," came the reply.

Septimus asked Darius, "And what of our fellow legionaries in Camulodunum?"

Darius looked gravely at the line of soldiers. "The town has been overrun with mass slaughter of its inhabitants and burnt to the ground. Some escaped by boat or horse and came to warn us. They say she commands a fearsome army of thousands who will show no mercy… so, it's essential that we keep a lookout and remember your training." With that, he moved along the line, giving encouragement to the others.

III

They didn't have long to wait. A steady buildup of warriors on foot and a dozen war chariots soon filled the horizon. One chariot moved slowly forward along the road, stopping short of a defiant javelin-thrower's missile. A fearsome, white-bearded druid raged whilst holding up two severed heads of luckless Romans.

"Most likely officers from Camulodunum," Septimus wryly observed.

"Poor bastards," Marcellus muttered. "That druid looks in the mood for more slaughter."

"We don't need to know what he's saying. We get the message," Septimus grinned, running his fingers along the edge of his sword. He was always up for a fight. Marcellus was less sure and quietly hoped that Julia and Cato were safe and that Androgeus would remain loyal. He looked down the line and met the eye of Lupus in the next section, giving him a cheeky wave.

Septimus saw the exchange and laughed. "If all hell breaks loose, you might just get the chance to settle your debt."

Darius shouted a command and they each picked up a large rock from the baskets placed at intervals as a tide of painted warriors rushed screaming towards the enormous ditch. Scorpions unleashed their long, iron-tipped arrows on the mob, and the legionaries cheered as they punched holes through flimsy shields and the bodies behind of surprised warriors.

"Wait till they're in the ditch!" Darius yelled.

As the first line jumped down and started to scramble up the side, the legionaries threw rocks on them, continuing until the first wave of attackers had withdrawn. Stragglers were picked off by javelin-throwers as slaves replenished their rock baskets. From the gatehouse roof, a catapult sent a huge, iron-tipped spear flying towards the druid's chariot, striking it with force and killing the driver. The druid managed to jump out, eliciting loud cheers from the defenders.

"His gods didn't warn him of that!" Marcellus laughed, throwing a rock at a determined, blue-painted warrior. Few wore helmets, and their dark brown mops of hair made appealing targets for the legionaries.

But their numbers were huge - it was surely a coming together of many tribes, each with different coloured braids in their hair and designs painted on their round, cowhide shields. All were naked to the waist, men and women, with their faces and torsos painted with blue swirls. Waves of yelling warriors kept running at the ditch and scrambling up the bank, exhausting the soldiers' supplies of javelins, rocks, and any other objects they could throw. The small scorpions and larger catapults caused more carnage at their rear ranks, but not enough to make them fall back.

A cry went up to the east of Marcellus. A group of fifteen warriors were trying to remove an iron portcullis beneath a wooden frame that was protecting an opening where a stream ran through their defences. Some determined warriors had survived the barrage of rocks and javelins and attached a rope to the gate, and a chariot was now trying to pull it out.

Darius made up a squad of twenty men to run out through the gate and remove the threat. Marcellus watched from the platform as they formed into a turtle formation, holding their shields to all sides and over the heads of the unit as they jogged past grave markers towards the chariot. Warriors threw themselves against the Roman shields, scornfully kicking aside wooden grave markers and urns of ashes, some recoiling with stab wounds for their efforts.

Soon Darius and his men reached the chariot and fighting broke out to cheers from the bank. Darius slew the occupants and cut the horse loose. He ordered the chariot be pushed over before organising his men into two lines to fight their way back to the gate as greater numbers of enraged warriors began to surround them. The legionaries jogged in formation, smashing their shield bosses into enraged warriors or stabbing them with their spears.

Centurion Maximius, the garrison commander, was a cautious man who rebuffed entreaties from some of his optios to send a second unit out to cover their retreat. One by one, the soldiers were cut down and hacked with axes, swords, and knives, or bludgeoned with hammers. The mood on the platform changed as soldiers groaned at seeing their comrades killed off. The fearsome warrior Darius was the last to fall, surrounded by a dozen screaming savages who literally tore him to pieces. His head was crudely severed and held aloft in triumph by howling warriors.

"Well, that didn't work," Septimus sneered. His grimace revealed his contempt for their centurion who visibly recoiled in horror, betraying the lack of steely resolve that was expected of a commander at war.

The momentum was now with the Britons and they surged forward, their leaders realising that the garrison was undermanned and the Romans had thrown all their rocks and javelins, and fired all their bolts. They had picked up the Romans' lightweight, iron javelins to supplement their own weapons, some put on the helmets of the fallen, as they avoided the deadly gatehouse platform and charged through the ditch and onto the flimsy defences beyond. The legionaries had sturdy, wooden iron-tipped spears and swords for close combat and set about a desperate defence of the inadequate earth bank defence.

Marcellus and Septimus were soon embroiled in hand-to-hand fighting as dozens of shrieking attackers jumped onto their section of the shaky wooden platform.

"Their women are as fierce as the men!" Septimus shouted above the noise of battle, impaling a screaming female warrior on his spear.

"Ouch!" Marcellus yelped, as a small stone from a sling hit his cheek strap. "What is it about this damned island that breeds such violent people?" He slashed and stabbed at the next wild-eyed demon before him. A trumpet blast announced the order to fall back. They looked to the gatehouse to see Maximius shouting his orders and pointing his sword towards the picket fence surrounding the barracks. The groaning soldiers complied, knowing it was a premature decision to abandon the outer perimeter. Once inside, the blue-painted warriors ran screaming to the gates and opened them so their chariots could enter.

"The town is lost!" Septimus shouted as they fought their way backwards, trying to maintain a solid line of rectangular shields, thrusting with spears at their crazed enemy. They were sorely missing Darius's sound judgement; the other optios in their cohort lacked his campaign experience, and they knew Centurion Maximius was more of a career politician than military leader, with little stomach for a fight.

Septimus seemed to sense what his friend was thinking and said, "I suggest we ignore the command to defend the barracks and head for the port."

Marcellus grinned and nodded. The fighting was getting more intense, and they saw their opportunity for mutiny when their nearest optio, an aged soldier just months from retirement, fell to a hammer blow. They were now outside the site of a planned amphitheatre, demarcated by a flimsy, circular wooden fence.

The distressed trumpeting of the town's curiosity, an old elephant named Valeria after one of the Emperor Claudius's wives, could be heard as it broke through the wooden fencing of the amphitheatre where it lived. It had served its purpose of carrying Claudius from Londinium to Camulodunum some fifteen years earlier, and was left behind by the departing imperial fleet. The soldiers eyed it with cautious glances over their shoulders as they edged backwards along the street, whilst its handler, a tiny and equally old dark-skinned man, beat it with a stick and shouted instructions in a harsh language. The mighty beast bellowed once more and turned away from the retreating soldiers towards the river.

"On me!" yelled Septimus, as he broke the line and ran after the elephant down a street of two-storey townhouses. He was older than most of the soldiers, a veteran of three campaigns, and his voice conveyed authority. In the absence of any officers in the vicinity, the twenty or so survivors of their unit ran after him. The street emptied into a wide square, full of frantic townsfolk, many pushing carts loaded with possessions towards the wooden bridge over the stream that dissected the settlement. Valeria and her rider cut a wide channel through the terrified crowd and, ignoring the bridge, headed for the warehouses that lined the port.

Septimus formed up the men into two ranks of ten, covering the width of the narrow street where it met the square, to buy time for as many people as possible to cross the bridge. The front rank held their shields out in front, with spears poking out between them, and the rear rank held their shields up, tilted over the heads of their comrades. They held their position, blocking the entrance to the square, whilst letting a few civilians squeeze past. Seconds later, a hoard of screaming warriors hurled themselves on the wall of shields, all coming off worse with either fatal or debilitating stab wounds to show for their zeal. The chastened natives regrouped halfway up the street, eying their enemy with suspicion. One of their chiefs appeared and shouted a command. They turned and ran back the way they had come to look for an alternative route through the town.

The legionaries cheered and struck their spears on their shields in celebration of this minor victory. "Jogging in ranks of two!" Septimus ordered, as he led his unit across the square towards the approach to a narrow bridge that divided the town. This had become a funnel for the desperate townsfolk and soldiers trying to escape the mad slaughter behind them. It was a natural place to make a stand against their enemy, as the bridge was the centrepiece of the main east to west road, the *Via Decumena*, that connected the two main hills on which the original camps had been established. Now, it divided the town from the port. Septimus positioned his men at either side of the approach to the bridge and grabbed at deserters, telling them to form up in a line with his men under pain of death.

"We shall cover the escape of our citizens!" Septimus shouted, looking magnificent beneath a statue of Hercules. Agitated townsfolk were making their way towards the cluster of soldiers in the hope of salvation from both directions along the wide, cobblestoned road. Abandoned carts littered the road, providing obstacles around which fleeing townsfolk navigated.

Septimus had secured the services of twenty additional soldiers and his unit successfully held off the baying attackers for a short while, allowing dozens of terrified people to cross the rickety wooden bridge. They ran on, through narrow streets, dodging startled livestock, past shrines, shops and imperial buildings towards the docks. The soldiers started to edge backwards across the bridge in two ranks, as Marcellus worked with two engineers underneath to tie ropes around the wooden supports. Septimus held the middle of the bridge for as long as possible, but the blue hordes were growing in number and some warriors had flung themselves into the brook and started to wade across.

"Let's go!" he yelled. "Pull away!"

Marcellus had tied the ropes around a couple of auxiliary cavalrymen's horses and, together with as many men as he could muster, pulled at the support beams until they succeeded in toppling the bridge with an almighty crash.

"That will slow them down a bit," Septimus growled. "Come on."

They followed the fleeing citizens past the temples to Jupiter and Fortuna -familiar places of worship to the legionaries - onwards past deserted market stalls and empty corrals, out into a wide, open square in the centre of the port. Imposing imperial buildings stood on two sides, some still under construction, and they headed for the walled enclosure that housed the procurator's opulent villa. Townsfolk were running and screaming, being chased and butchered by Briton warriors who cared not if their victims were Roman or fellow islanders. To add to the chaos, the elephant and some terrified horses were running amok, knocking anyone in their path aside like skittles.

"To the procurator's residence!" Septimus shouted above the din, pointing with his gladius as the troops, whose number had dwindled to barely thirty, jogged in formation past dead and dying people, occasionally slashing at screaming painted warriors as they went. They ran through an unguarded gate and up a flight of marble stairs, under the impassive, stone gaze of Jupiter and Augustus Caesar, to find the big double doors barred to them. Marcellus banged his sword hilt on the door and demanded to be let in. Septimus formed the men into a semicircle at the top of the stairs, flanked on both ends by tall Corinthian columns, then joined Marcellus at the doors.

"What next, my brother?" he panted.

Marcellus replied, "I remember from guard duty that this door is barred by one beam sitting on two brackets. If we can try to raise the beam…"

The two friends set about wedging a spear through the gap between the doors and under the beam, straining to work the heavy lump of wood upwards. The fighting was intensifying at the top of the stairs behind them as they slowly worked the stubborn lump of wood up and shook it from its brackets. With a loud thud it fell to the floor, and they pushed open the heavy doors.

"Let's get the men inside quickly and re-brace the door," Septimus muttered. They picked up their shields and spears and stood either side of the open doorway.

"Fall back!" Septimus yelled at the backs of his men. Half a dozen had fallen, but the remaining twenty-or-so edged back and through the doors. "Marcellus, have the beam ready!"

It was no easy manoeuvre as the Britons were battling fiercely around the doorway. Septimus and five men defended the opening, falling back incrementally until their comrades were able to force the doors shut in the faces of the angry mob. Marcellus and another soldier worked the beam back down into its brackets. For a brief moment, they stood in the cool, shadowy space to catch their breath and take in the majesty of the enormous hall lined with columns supporting the high roof. Marcellus noted Diana leading a deer hunt in a painted mural on one wall and the gods on Mount Olympus adorned the ceiling. They ran over an intricate, tiled mosaic of Medusa in the centre of the floor, her snake-hair hissing defiantly at the intruders.

"I'm not a citizen, sir, merely a humble soldier. I shouldn't be here," muttered the awe-struck young auxiliary at Marcellus' side.

The men around them shared a laugh at his worry about breaking a civil code, lightening the moment.

"Today, I am Caesar," Septimus declared, placing his hand on the young man's shoulder, "and I give you all permission to enter my hall. Now, come on." The grinning soldiers raced across the deserted space, past upturned tables and chairs, golden candlesticks, and incense burners littering the floor. They passed through a series of small rooms at the end of the hall which bore all the signs of a hurried evacuation.

A single door led the way out into a walled garden, lined with statues of gods, goddesses, glorious Caesars, and a new, shiny white one of Nero, their current emperor. The soldiers couldn't help but gawp at this sacred and off-limits garden where generals, governors, and provincial administrators had sat on marble benches to make their plans for the submission of the wild province of Britannia. A gate at the south end of the garden was being guarded by two surprised Praetorians. After a word from Septimus, the soldiers were let through into the chaotic scene at the port of Londinium.

IV

The dockside was a mass of jostling and shouting people; sailors and slaves carrying a variety of imperial objects aboard three galleys, and lesser traders filling a dozen or so small boats with people and supplies. In the distance, Marcellus noticed the elephant entering the river to swim into the current. He looked around to try and get a sight of his wife, Julia, but couldn't see her amongst the throng of townsfolk desperate to find a boat or get onto the bridge.

"Watch where you're going!" a citizen being carried on a sedan chair shouted, whacking Androgeus on the head with a leather whip, causing him to stagger, as the jostling tide of humanity made their way to a row of moored boats on the quayside.

"Do not abuse my slave, sir!" Julia shouted above the din. "My husband is a legionary fighting for our safety." She hugged her child tightly and glared at the fat, impassive Patrician.

Androgeus turned and grinned his appreciation at his plucky mistress. "This way, my lady - Petronius the wine merchant has a boat. Your husband is a regular customer of his, he'll help us. Let us make haste." They battled through the anxious crowd as the distant sounds of battle grew increasingly louder. Androgeus had briefly considered abandoning his charges to escape and join the revolt but decided against it when a friend told him that many of their own tribe had been slaughtered at Camulodunum. They were regarded as appeasers of the hated Romans by those with grievances to settle. He needed to be in the same boat as his masters.

Marcellus searched the crowd again for Julia and Cato but couldn't see them amongst the multitude of milling townsfolk and soldiers. He did see Procurator Decianus and Centurion Maximius standing on the prow of a galley, the latter bellowing out orders for a defensive square. Legionaries with shields and weapons intact started to move towards the outer edges of the square and stand side by side, awaiting the barbarian onslaught.

Septimus grabbed Marcellus by the arm and pointed to a small boat that was already bobbing freely in the river. On it, Julia and Cato were shouting and waving to them, their words snatched away by the breeze and hubbub. A broad smile cracked Marcellus' cheeks as he waved back, relief etched on his blood-spattered face.

"Now we can fight barbarians," he said, grinning at his friend. Septimus called his unit into a huddle and left them to go in search of a friendly sea captain. But no sooner was he gone than a boisterous optio commanded them to form up in the defensive wall. Marcellus duly complied with the rest of the unit, and they found themselves with members of the first cohort who hadn't yet faced the enemy as they'd been guarding the docks and both ends of the bridge.

"What's it like?" one of them asked the cut, bleeding, and battered unit.

Marcellus replied, "Imagine thousands of blue-painted screaming devils being chased through the Gates of Hades by the three-headed hound Cerberus. Look - here they come...!" He pointed with the tip of his gladius as the first group of warriors raced from the streets that fed into the open space before the docks, screaming and waving their bloody weapons. They stopped short of the wall of Roman shields and seemed to wait for one of their leaders to come. They shouted obscenities and banged their swords, spears, and axes against their round shields, and some threw the severed heads of soldiers and townsfolk at the Romans. The evacuation of non-combatants was swiftly completed and

Maximius, from the safety of his galley, urged them to hold the line at all costs.

"General Paulinius is on his way!" Maximius shrieked, his lie barely carrying above the racket to a doubtful Marcellus. No one was coming to save them.

The warriors then quietened and parted to allow three chariots to enter from a side street. The lead chariot held Boudica, a tall, proud woman with long, flowing red hair and blue swirls on her cheeks, wearing a shining metal breastplate and silver torque around her neck, and clutching a spear. She glared over the heads of the soldiers, pointing her spear at the hated procurator on the galley deck. She urged her driver to ride between the two lines of opposing soldiers, periodically throwing severed heads over the line of Roman shields as she went. Marcellus gazed at her in awe, her authority over the seemingly wild rabble was undisputed. Some even bowed as she rode by. She lifted her spear again and screamed a command as her chariot reached the end of the line, and her faithful followers fell on the Roman shield wall with maddening ferocity.

The line held. The second ranks stabbed with their spears and the front ranks jabbed with their short swords. The enraged Britons pulled back to see their fallen comrades lining the flagstones. Boudica led her three chariots to the back of her Briton army, and a pathway soon opened, giving her a clear run at the Roman shields. With a spine-chilling scream, again holding her spear aloft, she urged the three chariots into a full gallop straight at the unfortunate legionaries in their path, cutting through them with a loud clatter accompanied by the neighing of terrified horses and the screams of those battered, trampled, and stabbed in her wake. Her warriors flooded through the gap in the shield wall and the scene broke into desperate hand-to-hand fighting between Londinium's defenders and Briton warriors.

Marcellus and his unit had become a band of brothers, looking out for each other as they fought on the eastern edge of the docks. Through the melee he spotted the hulking figure of Brutus and knew Lupus would be close by - they had abandoned the fighting and were making for a boat moored at the quayside. No doubt Lupus had used some of his hoard of coins to arrange his escape. Just then, Septimus appeared at Marcellus' side.

"I've secured a boat under the first arch of the bridge and paid a slave to wait for my return," he said. "If I fall, that's where you must go to be reunited with your family."

"Neither of us shall fall," Marcellus replied through gritted teeth, felling a skinny, old man with a balding head and few teeth. Two screaming bare-breasted women ran at them, and easily batted away their spear thrusts with their shields, stabbing out at the legionaries' bodies with their swords. The women were wise to the Roman moves, as were all who had survived one-on-one combat with a legionary. Septimus went on the offensive and drove his shield into his opponent's face - the round, metal boss breaking her nose - and then plunged his gladius into her belly. Marcellus then swiftly finished off her distracted and enraged friend.

"Maybe they were sisters," he said, adding, "I take little pleasure in fighting women."

"Anyone with a weapon is fair game to me," the muscular Spaniard replied, "although it pains me to kill young boys in whose faces I see my dead son." The battle, however, was not going well for the Romans who were falling back to the quayside and jumping into boats and the one remaining moored galley upstream of the bridge.

"Let's go," Septimus said, indicating for the unit, now down to just ten, to follow him. They fought their way to the edge of the quay and slipped in single file along a narrow pathway that led under the bridge. Sturdy tree trunks had been driven into the muddy riverbed and thick planks of wood linked the uprights to support a thin wooden platform. A unit of Romans guarding the approach to the bridge were now engaged in fighting off a barbarian onslaught - the battle raged above them, and the occasional body fell into the river as Septimus, Marcellus and their eight surviving comrades boarded the rocking vessel. Marcellus steadied himself on the central mast as Septimus took the tiller from a grinning, fawning slave and moved the boat out into the current, the six oarsmen quickly pulling away from the chaotic dockside.

V

The battle was lost and the galley carrying the procurator, centurion and several hundred men had cast off. It was still upstream of the bridge, heading for the wider centre span where a drawbridge was being opened for the high central mast to pass through. Marcellus and his comrades watched the drama unfold as a desperate defence of the raised bridge was put up by a band of plucky legionaries as screaming warriors poured onto the shaking bridge. The warriors overpowered and killed the few remaining guards and some terrified civilians and cut away the ropes that held up their leaf of the raised bridge, sending it crashing down, but too late to prevent the galley passing through. There was little they could do apart from shout abuse and hurl what few weapons and objects came to hand. The Romans shielded themselves and shouted abuse back, passing safely into the widening river estuary.

Septimus pointed to a boat ahead of them as the general melee started to fade behind them. "That's your friend, Lupus, and the brute, Brutus." The six oarsmen rowed them alongside the smaller boat and Septimus shouted a friendly, "Hail fellow legionaries of the Ninth!" The other boat returned the welcome and threw a rope so the two boats could join. Lupus saw Marcellus and let out a low growl.

"Do you have a problem with one of us?" Septimus asked him.

"Indeed," Lupus replied, "one of your good men owes me a debt." He pointed to Marcellus.

"My comrade Marcellus tells me that you threatened him and his wife if the debt wasn't paid. Is that right?" Septimus challenged him.

"It's no business of yours, my friend," the impish soldier replied.

"What if I said that I will take my friend's debt on, and that you should look to me for repayment?"

Lupus scowled and Brutus started to stand. "Then you owe me four denarii, soldier," he said.

"But I hear your dice are weighted and you make your money by cheating soldiers out of their hard-earned pay. Show me your dice and I will roll them," Septimus replied.

Brutus made to board the boat, but Septimus was ready for him, moving swiftly to grab his arm as the boats rocked in the swell. The big man swayed with the unsteady motion of the boat and Septimus threw him headlong into the river. Those with surplus energy cheered whilst others made crude gestures, but Lupus moved to cut the rope holding the boats together. Marcellus quickly jumped on him, twisting his arm behind his back.

"Arrgh ... get off! You'll pay for this!" he screeched. By now, all the others were laughing at this much-welcomed entertainment after such a harrowing and bloody battle. Marcellus wrenched the dice from Lupus's purse and handed them to Septimus. Some of the men were slumped on the floor and reluctant to move, but a few gathered around as Septimus rolled one, then the other. Soon, a pattern was emerging that was all too obvious - now they were aware of the ruse. Septimus tore off the parchment coating to reveal a thin, iron plate on one side of each wooden cube.

"I see. This metal strip adds weight to one side making it heavier and therefore the number on the opposite side will show more often. Very sly. So, you are a cheat and must repay all those who've been cheated by you. Bring me his bag."

As Lupus wriggled, Septimus found a large bag of coins in his backpack.

"Well, Lupus, should we find out how well you swim, or will you concede to being exposed as a cheat and pay back your victims?" Septimus trailed his hand in the murky waters. "And I must say, it's very cold in there - just ask your friend Brutus." They all turned to see the big man swimming slowly to the shore some way behind them, looking very peeved. "This land is now a very unsafe place for Romans. What say you?"

Lupus glared at him and finally nodded his head. Marcellus let him go and caught the bag of coins Septimus threw him.

"Take your losses and distribute the rest to any surviving dice players," Septimus ordered, drawing weary barks of laughter from the men. The galley had caught up with them and someone was shouting from the upper deck. It was the portly figure of their commanding officer, Centurion Maximius.

"What are you men laughing about?" he yelled. "We have lost this battle, and just surrendered our supply port in this damned island to the barbarians!"

Septimus stood and saluted his commander. "We mean no offence, sir. Let's just say we've resolved a minor dispute and it has cheered the men. I can assure you that these men of the second cohort of the Ninth Legion, who guarded the north bank, acquitted themselves with honour in the battle."

Maximius replied, "That is a fine speech, soldier. I saw how well your unit fought. You will come to my tent when we make landfall on Thanet. Hail Nero!"

They followed in the wake of the galley, going with the brown-grey flow of the impassive river, occasionally looking back to see Londinium burning, all red and orange flames, grey smoke spiralling to the skies. It was a funeral pyre for their fallen comrades, a show of utter contempt for the Roman invaders, exposing their weaknesses. It was an indication of the worthlessness of the settlement and all things Roman to the bold Britons who would soon wipe off their paint and melt away into the dark, foreboding forests or salty marshes.

"Are their gods stronger than ours?" Marcellus groaned at the sight of a legionary slipping under the brown, choppy flow as two tribal warriors up to their knees in muddy slime pointed their spears and shouted curses.

"Their flesh-eating god, Tamesis, will grow fat feeding on our brothers," Septimus sourly replied. "But our generals will return with a greater force to subdue this stubborn island for the lumps of lead and silver in their rocks."

Marcellus grunted and pulled on an oar, joining a flotilla of boats that followed in the wake of the galley. "Then, I hope they rebuild their towns with high stone walls, as these painted devils have had the taste of victory."

A Summer's Disquiet

"That smirk of yours will be your end."

Low beams bowed in on the White Hart tavern's dirt floor with the threat of collapse on the heads of a dozen oblivious patrons. Farm labourers mixed with pilgrims now just a day's ride from Canterbury and the holy relic of Saint Thomas à Becket. One such pilgrim gasped at the sight of a burly local holding a knife to the throat of a bulging-eyed man whose back was pinned to an upturned barrel.

"If I says Edward the Black Prince himself pressed a groat into my 'and after we slaughtered them Frenchies at Poitiers, then it 'appened, you miserable toad," the knife man hissed, his dark-eyed stare conveying murderous intent.

The terrified customer recoiled from his assailant's blade and sour breath; his eyes fixed on a scar that shone white through pox-marked skin.

"Now, now, Wat, he don't doubt you. Let him up now, 'twere just a misunderstanding... there are God-fearing pilgrims under my roof." A hand on the knife man's shoulder seemed to suck the malice from him.

Wat Tyler eased his blade away from the quivering man's stubble and slowly turned to face the landlord. "You know the truth, Bill. I may 'ave been little more than a boy at that great battle, but I was there."

"Yes, you were, Wat. Now settle your tab and be on your way."

With a grunt, the old soldier tossed a couple of pennies bearing the head of the great King Edward III who had died just four years earlier on a table and walked out of the gloom into the bright light of late afternoon to find a crowd had gathered around the water pump at the centre of the village square. It was June 1381, and the crops were sprouting well in the warming days of summer.

Wat stood back to let a pair of Shire horses plod towards their stable, a boy of barely twelve years flicking the reins that directed the huge beasts. He fingered a small leather pouch around his neck at the sight of the boy who was about the same age as his own son when he had died of the black death.

"What's 'appening 'ere?" he asked a milkmaid struggling by with two full pails balanced on the ends of a yoke across her shoulders.

"It's a travellin' preacher, sir," she mumbled. "A holy man, some say…"

Wat marched towards the crowd to listen to the speaker, stepping carefully to avoid the dung and rotting cabbage cores. The tall, tonsured stranger held his audience in thrall to him with a deep, powerful voice that commanded attention, allied to the wide sweeps of his arms as if dispensing blessings on the heads of the peasants.

"…It is less than two hundred years since King John sealed a great charter of freedom that says all men shall have rights to live without fear of unjust punishment or imprisonment on the whim of their lord. But now, those of you who, by God's grace and favour, have survived the black plague, now find yourselves bound to the service of your lord who refuses to pay you what you deserve for your labour. Nor will he grant you permission to move elsewhere to earn more on farms where the pestilence took too many…"

The preacher paused to let his words sink in and view the bowed heads of the pious assembly who crossed themselves in thanks for their deliverance. The ties of the feudal system were firmly embedded after three hundred years of Norman rule and remained strong, he knew, and it would take much to rouse them to cross their liege lord who had the power to ruin or imprison them at will. But they were trapped by more than their feudal obligations: the passing of the seasons, the festivals, and saints' day rituals, tied them all to the rhythm of village life.

"But that's not all," he continued. "Our fine and greedy nobles have now passed a law to collect taxes directly from you, the workers who till this land, that will take much of your hard-earned coin. They are calling it a poll tax as all workers who are named in the rolls of the Doomsday Book will not escape having to pay up. Our landowning bishops sit in parliament with the nobility, and they also voted for this wicked tax on you, the hard-working common folk still reeling with grief from loved ones lost to the great plague."

At this, the crowd were roused to groans and moans of angry disquiet. Wat Tyler was impressed and pushed his way through the mob to stand in front of the sturdy preacher who was standing on an upturned wooden box. Wat looked up at the fervent, plain-clothed man, an agemate who had seen around forty summers, as he developed his theme of man's rights to be treated with fairness and to push for equality in all dealings with both Church and Lord.

"But we shall be imprisoned if we defy our Lord!" a man shouted from behind Wat.

The old soldier turned to regard his ruddy-faced neighbour. They lived in a row of thatched stone cottages, merely two rooms to each abode that let in little light. Wat worked during the day as a tanner in a shed next to the abattoir, soaking and pounding cow hides with a large, wooden mallet to thin layers that would be sold to passing merchants. His wife, Maggie, worked as a cowherd and milkmaid on the estate of their lord, Thomas Holland, Earl of Kent. They all had to drop to one knee and remove their hats whenever their lord rode by. Holland was a humourless man who rarely spoke the English language and meted out justice once a month at a local court. Wat had been punished many times for minor discourtesies and had felt the lash of the sheriff's man's whip on his back. He, a proud old soldier, who had fought for King Edward in his French wars.

"I have just in these past two days been released from the archbishop's prison, for God the Almighty knew I was falsely accused for doing His work!" the preacher yelled. "Fear not the wrath of those who do you wrong. God sees all and you shall bathe in the warm glow of his good grace."

Wat was impressed. This quietened the crowd, whose mood seemed to shift from one of the dull compliance of prisoners to people roused to anger at the injustices heaped on them. He waited until the preacher had finished his sermon, then removed his hat and bowed his head for the final prayer and blessing.

"In God we trust," Wat muttered under his breath. He knew the power of the Church allied to the authority of the nobility under a king who ruled by divine right were formidable masters of men's hearts and minds. It was a yoke he would love to break.

"May I have a word, Father?" Wat asked the preacher as he stepped down from his box.

"Yes, my child. What is it that you wish to know?" His question conveyed the assumption that Wat was a humble penitent seeking spiritual guidance.

Wat drew himself to his full height, on a par with the tall preacher, and looked him in the eye. "I find myself in agreement with your views on how us ordinary folk are subjected to a life of toil and misery for a handful of coins that barely pay for our food and shelter. And now this tax on us is announced, we must protest at this injustice. But to whom shall we protest?" He turned and raised his shirt to show the welts on his back from the lash.

The preacher raised his eyebrows at the sight. "I see that you have incurred the wrath of your lord." He regarded Wat for a moment. "May I ask what you work at, my son?"

"I'm a tanner but was once a soldier in King Edward's army. May I know your name, Father? I'm Wat Tyler."

"I am John Ball, a priest without a parish, ever since I fell afoul of the archbishop. He does not like me stirring up discontent amongst his flock in this diocese of Kent."

Wat grinned before responding. "P'raps the time is right for discontent with this new tax on us workers, added to the fact that our workload has increased owing to so many having perished in the plague. We are few and our labour must surely command better pay…"

"I know little about demands for better pay, master Tyler, but I chime with you on the rights of ordinary folk to make their grievances known without fear of punishment, in the hope that their conditions may improve, or their suffering be alleviated. In God's eyes, we are all equal and our immortal souls are in His care."

"Then we are in agreement, Father. I believe the time has come for us to take our grievances to our earthly masters and demand fairer conditions and pay. P'raps we could join forces to spread this message of hope to the people?"

It was John Ball's turn to grin. "I have heard it has already started, in Essex across the estuary from us. There are uprisings going on as we speak. As word spreads, it may prove easier to stir our people here in Kent. Let's talk more on this, master Tyler. I believe that the Almighty is guiding me to bring succour to his people who have endured much these past years."

Men touched their caps in deference to the preacher as the crowd dispersed, peasant labourers in the main, returning to their homes as the last rays of the sun filtered through a screen of trees that bordered one side of the village.

John Ball suddenly tensed and looked over Wat's shoulder. The old soldier turned to see the sheriff and his two men come riding into the square. They were too late to break up the gathering but would surely be looking for the travelling rabble-rouser.

"Follow me, Father Ball, to my cottage beyond those trees. You can share our supper and bed down for the night." Wat grabbed the priest by his elbow and hurriedly led him between two rows of cottages and away from the roving eyes of the sheriff's men.

*****

The Aldgate, one of three stone gatehouses that marked the mid-points of the London wall that bounded the city of London on three sides, the fourth side being the river front, was the destination for the Mayor of London, William Walworth. He nudged his horse past the street sellers and dodged the hand- or horse-pulled carts piled high with goods entering the city or waste leaving it for the dump pits beyond the gate. Having handed the reins to an eager stableboy, he mounted the stone steps to a row of modest apartments that stood above the gatehouse and knocked the iron ring on the second door along the walkway.

"Ah, William!" a slight, greying man with round spectacles exclaimed upon opening the door. "Do come in."

Once the oak door had closed on the yells, brays, and squawks of London life below, William removed his brimmed felt hat and greeted his friend. "Ah, Geoffrey, it's been a while. So, these are your new rooms. Very... compact, my learned friend." His eyes swept over the room, adjusting to the gloom, and came to rest on a parchment-strewn desk by the window with two feathered quills protruding from an inkwell. "My apologies for dragging you from your desk. Will you write more humorous tales of mischievous pilgrims? I rather enjoyed your Miller's tale. My father was a miller, you know."

Geoffrey Chaucer led the way to a pair of worn armchairs and beckoned his friend to sit. "My dear William, your visit is a welcome distraction from my writing desk, as my shoulders and eyes are in need of respite. Yes, you told me anecdotes from your childhood that fed my febrile imagination. But now the fishmonger has risen to the office of Mayor, come and tell me of your worries and what news of these Essex rebellions that are on the lips of the street gossips." Despite not yet reaching forty years, the slight, timid figure, was already hunched and greying, but remained a firm favourite at the court of the boy-king, Richard, who enjoyed the celebrity author's fanciful storytelling.

William sat heavily and puffed his vexation. "It's bad, my dear friend, and I come to warn you that a mob from Essex, having burned their towns and killed some of our tax collectors, are on the march and shall soon pass through this gate."

Chaucer let out a groan. "But can you not bar them from entering the city?"

"We lack the manpower, and King Richard has ordered the nobles within to assemble at the Tower with as many men as they can muster. The king's guard number barely a hundred and his uncle, Gaunt, is still in the north fighting the Scots and quelling the northern rebellions. I fear we are caught, Geoffrey, ill-prepared, and to make matters worse, we now hear that the men of Kent are gathering at Blackheath. I must hurry to the Tower but have come to beseech you to join me, for your safety."

Chaucer's rheumy eyes roved over his desk then back to his wealthy friend, his bony knuckles shone white on locked fingers. "The rebels will surely pass beneath me without disturbance, William, and I am better placed here for a swift exit should they occupy our city. Thank you for your offer, but I shall remain with my dusty books and record what I see."

William let out a sigh and stood. "Then I shall take my leave. I must dismiss my household and pack a saddlebag for an indefinite stay at the Tower of London. Two rebel armies descending on us will number in their thousands, and we appear to be helpless before their ire."

Chaucer also rose to shake his friend's hand. "If John of Gaunt were here, then he would lead the king's men. But he is not… Good luck to you, William. You may find yourself leading the negotiations with the rebels. I shall pray that good sense and reason prevails."

*****

Wat Tyler and John Ball wore grins as they led their ragged army of over a thousand men bearing farming implements for weapons through the streets of Southwark where cheering residents waved from the windows and open doorways. More joined them to swell their ranks and make a merry carnival of defiance as they called a halt at the approach to London Bridge, surprised that no armed guard opposed them. Instead, townsfolk cheered from the windows of upper floors of the buildings that lined both sides of the wide bridge.

"We have the support of the commoners, and God is with us," John Ball shouted above the din of raucous laughter and cheering. On their journey from the village, they released prisoners from the jails and burned all the court records they had found in the homes of magistrates and court officials, thwarting as they saw it, the chance of re-arrest and reprisals should the natural order return in the aftermath of their rebellion.

They had drafted a document whose terms they had shouted at the wary king and his courtiers at a bizarre meeting that very morning on the river. King Richard, now a youth of 14 years, had fidgeted nervously on his throne on the royal barge that bobbed a safe distance from the muddy riverbank as his nobles and archbishops exchanged cautious words with Wat and John. The rebel leaders had refused to disperse the mob and return to their homes, saying they would present their charter in person to the king in London.

"We've crossed the king, Wat," John Ball said, as he laid his hands on the head of a kneeling woman.

"Aye, and our fate is no doubt sealed as traitors if we do not succeed in changing the order of things. But we shall still move on the Tower of London and lay siege to it until they agree to our terms. Did you see the look of dismay on their faces at the size of our army?"

"It's the only reason they have agreed to receive our document and study it." Wat betrayed his anxiety to the priest by fingering the pouch around his neck.

"May I ask what token that pouch contains? P'raps the bone of a saint?" John Ball enquired.

Wat turned to his friend and grinned. "It contains locks of hair from my boy and girl, who both died writhing in pain from the black death. I can't forget the memory of their little bodies a mass of blisters and black buboes, the feeling of helplessness... My Maggie and I wept until we 'ad no more tears. I'm doing this for them, and those of us who survived the plague. That we may have justice and the rights promised us by the charter of freedom you spoke of."

They crossed the bridge and swarmed towards the Tower of London, setting up camp in the vacant land that surrounded the imposing fortress and symbol of Norman power. They were not the first to arrive, and a thick-armed brute approached Wat and introduced himself as Jack Straw, leader of the Essex rebels.

"Well met, friend," Tyler exclaimed, shaking the brute firmly by the hand whilst maintaining eye contact, keen to impress on him that he was the natural leader. The three sat, and soon Ball and Tyler had entranced the illiterate Straw with their list of demands, written on parchment by the priest.

"We intend to demand a meeting with King Richard and personally present him with our demands for reform. We shall stand steadfast and true to our cause, for God is with us!" Ball proclaimed, gaining cheers from those who were loitering around.

"You are both preacher and prophet!" the slightly overwhelmed Straw replied, turning to his followers to lead them in a raucous cheer.

Tyler grinned, enjoying his moment of power based on sheer numbers over a clearly weak and ill-prepared government. More groups of rebellious common folk from surrounding towns and villages were joining them, until their numbers surpassed three thousand. Tyler was quick to call a council of leaders, identifying himself, Straw, and Ball as the leadership group, and appointing deputies from those in charge of the smaller groups. They would all wear red strips of cloth tied to their arm as badges of rank.

"We shall not harm ordinary folk," Tyler shouted above the din, "but instead target the mansions and palaces of the wealthy nobility, magistrates, and hated tax collectors for looting and burning of documents. We know who they are and where they live." He then signalled for a bound prisoner to be brought forward. "This 'ere is Sir John Newton, Keeper of Rochester Castle." He paused as a wave of boos and abuse ran around the assembly. "He shall be sent to the Tower in the morning to present our terms to the king."

Tyler hushed the chatter and moved to conclude the meeting. "I will lead a group of followers to the Savoy Palace, residence of the Duke of Lancaster, John of Gaunt, uncle and most influential adviser to the boy-king, and symbol of oppression to the commoners. Now come forward one by one, my loyal deputies and I shall tell you whose mansions to raid."

All around, a full fairground of festivities had sprung up in the glow of a series of bonfires as the evening gave way to night. Rowdiness and drunkenness set in as jugglers, magicians, and dancing bears entertained the crowd. Added to the mayhem were mystery plays and strolling players who told stories from the Bible. Preachers preached whilst plundered food and drink was distributed by a group of determined women. Sword and staff fights broke out and dog fights were hastily arranged between competing villages.

Small groups bearing burning torches marched off along the streets on missions to attack the houses of wealthy merchants and minor nobles, judges, and court officials. Furniture was piled up outside and fires were fed with parchment documents. Many residences were torched that night and the occupants were whipped along the streets. Some were killed by the angry mob whose bloodlust gave way to slaughter, those involved feeling they were beyond the reach of the law. Fine goods were paraded before the increasingly drunk mob, which included handicrafts, perfumes, delicate wood carvings, furs, and delicious fruits of different kinds from far-off countries along with spices, cheeses, flour, wine, and meats. Despite calls to share, barter trades soon took place and sporadic fighting broke out. Bullies would not be denied the best of things plundered from their betters.

On Tyler's return from having burnt down the Savoy Palace, he witnessed the wondrous scene of a summer fayre, and laughed at a row of severed heads displayed on spikes as small dogs jumped to savour the bloody drips and strips of gore. "I'm sure that one's the warden of Newgate Prison!" he bawled, pointing.

"Aye, sir," a ruffian replied. "And we let out the prisoners who have joined us."

"And did you burn the records?"

"Aye, sir, and it made a pretty fire."

Wat put his head back and laughed loud and long. His followers joined in, prompting a small crowd to gather to witness the grisly sight.

*****

From the stone battlements of the Tower, William Walworth and his friends and fellow courtiers, Philipot, Brembre and Launde, looked on with anger and contempt.

"God's teeth! Those savages laugh at their handiwork as they gather round the heads of our loyal officers displayed on spikes. This is intolerable!" Walworth picked a spec of ash from his tongue and spat as Brembre patted his back.

"'Tis the laugh of Satan welcoming the damned at the gates of Hell," Philipot muttered, gripping his sword hilt as if in readiness to break up the ghastly celebration.

Others beside them, most notably the Archbishop of Canterbury and bishop of Southwark, crossed themselves and groaned. Archers lolled about, whispering in groups of three or four around burning braziers in the cooling night air.

"This madness may be dressed up as a protest against taxation and servitude, but it has now shown its true hand." Orange glows and smoke trails from burning buildings dotted the horizon, like an apocalyptic warning of doom. "We must advise our king to send out his guards to attack them whilst they are drunk and in the act of fornication," he added.

"Aye," Brembre added, "'tis our homes that are burning and our loyal officers whose heads are now displayed. This lawless behaviour is exactly why the common man must be kept down at heel, like a whippet."

"But we do not have an army at our disposal!" Archbishop Sudbury, squealed. "I fear we have gone too far with this taxation and keeping them down at heel. God is judging us harshly…" His words died out to a whisper.

"God is on the side of our King Richard, who rules by divine right. Are you doubting that, archbishop?" Walworth said, turning on the fretful, elderly man.

The king's cousin, Henry of Derby, stepped forward. "Come, come, good sirs. Let us keep a united front in this matter. The dull dimwits still revere the king and his mother, Queen Joan. They regard her as a saint. They are the ones who can take the sting out of the mob's ire. The king is of the opinion that we must do what we can to persuade them to disperse, then we shall visit them with terrible retribution. But we may have to wait until our armies return from France and the North. Let us retire to the hall where we should set our minds to uplifting the spirits of our noble king."

*****

"Our young king and his giddy age-mates are full of excitement, as if it were a tournament we are going to," Walworth whispered to his friend, Brembre, riding next to him. They were behind the royal party in a long parade that had been cautiously cheered by a modest turnout of loyal townsfolk as it wound its way from the Tower through

London's streets, past churches of stone, but in the main, lined with wood and thatch dwellings. Evidence of rioting could not be ignored with smoke trails rising from the embers of split timbers and broken furniture strewn before a smattering of ransacked houses.

"You've done well, Sir William, in guiding our king to meet the rebels at Smithfield where, despite their greater numbers, they shall see the king, his nobles, and his knights arrayed in their armour and fine livery." A day earlier, the grateful king had knighted Walworth, Brembre, Philipot and Launde for their forthright advice and bravery in facing up to the rebels at the first meeting. Their growing influence at court as trusted advisers to the king would ensure more favours once this matter was dealt with.

The former fishmonger smiled as he rolled in his saddle, uncomfortable due to the body armour fitted beneath his finely woven blue garment belted at the waist by a thick leather belt from which hung a sword and dagger in ornate scabbards. The chain of office of Mayor of London also weighed heavily around his thick neck. "It's the most open space within the city and should it come to a charge by heavy horse, the mob will be scattered, regardless of its size. We have mustered barely three hundred mounted soldiers, archers, nobles and their retainers, but that is enough to command one side of the ground."

The royal cavalcade lined up along one side of the open, square space, a well-known meeting point for fairs, markets, and holiday tournaments of jousting and other entertainments. It was the site of cattle, sheep, and horse markets - a place where livestock was slaughtered, and traitors executed. But on this day, Saturday, 15th June 1381, King Richard was now summoning his subjects to meet with him, thus gaining the upper hand and asserting his position as their ruler. The royal party took their place in the middle of the line, flanked on either side by determined armour-clad soldiers carrying lances. Behind them stood a line of archers.

The rebel army had been emboldened by the king's timid showing the day before, where he had meekly agreed to action their reforms and, rather foolishly, gave his blessing to "traitors", those enemies of Tyler, Ball, and Straw, being hunted down by the mob. Now, after a full day of looting and murder, three thousand commoners filed onto the green field of Smithfield and faced their king and his soldiers. To their front sat Tyler, Straw, and Ball mounted on ponies.

King Richard stood in his stirrups and called Walworth to him. "Tell their leaders to come forth and meet me, Sir William," he announced.

Walworth bowed, turned his horse, and rode across the open space between the two groups. He had seen Tyler at close quarters when the mob had crossed London bridge, and rode towards him, inviting him to come forward and meet with the king.

Tyler, flanked by Ball and Straw, approached the king, and greeted him directly, as if meeting an old friend, to the astonishment and chagrin of Richard's nobles and courtiers. He dismounted and stepped forward, prompting King Richard to raise his hand to still restless nobles who moved to block the impudent commoner. The youthful king's clear, unblemished cheeks shone white, framed by shoulder length auburn locks kept in place by a circlet of gold. Despite the warmth of the day, he wore a red cloak of fine lambswool, with ermine collar. His calm and regal demeanour had a settling effect on all around.

In contrast, Tyler's scarred and weathered face cracked in a gap-toothed grin. He was from a world of grime and toil, a servile class who would never speak to his betters unless receiving instruction or answering a charge in court. But now he was talking to the king himself, and from a position of power. Even so, he removed his cap, but remained standing.

Tyler spotted his liege lord, Thomas Holland, to whom he was effectively tied in service, and gave a mock bow with a cheeky wink. A visibly shocked Holland then seemed to recognise the troublemaker he had ordered to be whipped some time before.

Spurring his horse forward, Holland thundered, "Villain! You are my man. I did not give you permission to leave my estate! Now I see the extent of your villainy, leading this unholy rebellion and having the gall to address your king…"

Richard held up his hand to cut short his relative's tirade. "Please, Thomas, restrain yourself. This man, Master Tyler, is here to present the grievances of the common folk. He may address me directly in this matter."

What followed was a carefully prepared, twenty-minute speech by Tyler, who began with a list of grievances, demanding an end to serfdom and the removal of the unpopular poll tax. The nobility sat in stunned and irate silence, but a remarkably calm Richard smiled benevolently and encouraged him to continue.

Wat puffed his chest and gathered his thoughts. He felt inspired, that his entire life had been preparation for this moment - leader of a rebel army that still harboured ambitions to replace the king and nobility and for him to rule over England as king of the commoners.

"Your majesty, we also demand an end to the nobility and the courts, with no more outlawry and punishments, except those meted out by the king himself. Furthermore, we demand an end to the hierarchy of the Church with just one bishop for the whole country, and their lands to be divided amongst the parishioners. We demand an end to being tied to the service of our lords and that all men must be free and equal to go about their business."

Silence followed as everyone looked to the young king for his reaction. Ball and Straw exchanged quizzical looks, as this last part had not been agreed beforehand. An inspired Tyler's mind had clearly drifted to fantastical and unrealistic notions.

Richard merely smiled and replied, "All these things shall be given as it is in my power to do so, save for the sovereignty of the Crown. Now, Master Tyler, our meeting is concluded, and you must disband your army and return to your homes."

There was another silence, as both parties contemplated what to do next. Tyler had been given an order by his king, so it was for him to react. The young king held his nerve and stared down the rebel leader, and for what seemed an age, silence held sway over the field. High above, the caw of a crow, circling in anticipation of an outbreak of violence, broke Tyler's solemn reflection.

Tyler turned and demanded a jug of water to quench his thirst. This was handed to him by Jack Straw, and Tyler rinsed his mouth and spat on the ground between him and the boy-king. The king's response was not what Tyler had expected, and in a fit of pique he mounted his pony and, pulling at the reins, making to turn away without asking for his king's leave. But a cry of "traitor and murderer!" from one of the royal retainers caused an irritated and angry Tyler to turn back and shout a threat to whoever had made the utterance. He then drew his dagger and waved it in the air.

This petulant and threatening gesture was the opportunity Walworth had been hoping for. It was one insult too many and he rode forward to confront Tyler. "Villain! I am arresting you for inciting rebellion and insulting the king!" the Mayor thundered, loud enough for all to hear across the wide Smithfield.

Tyler was set on a course from which he could not turn, and he lunged at his tormentor with his dagger, the blade glancing off the hidden armour beneath Sir William's robe. Walworth pulled out his own dagger and stabbed at Tyler's neck, drawing blood. A knight broke ranks and charged at Tyler, running his sword's blade through Tyler's guts, delivering a mortal wound.

Across the field, the rebel army stood in the shadow of elm trees in the evening gloom, not sure what they could see apart from an animated exchange between the two groups before the king. John Ball intervened by grabbing the reins of Tyler's pony and leading him away, the wounded man swaying but staying upright in his saddle. They returned to the rebel ranks to be greeted with groans and angry oaths.

King Richard again intervened in events with a remarkable calmness and clarity of purpose. He held back his knights and nobles as they prepared for a full-scale cavalry charge at the rebels. Instead, he ordered Sir William to lead a group of soldiers in rounding up all fighting men who would come to support the king from the city, whilst he would continue to urge the rebels to disperse.

Barely an hour later, Sir William returned to Smithfield, surprised to see it deserted. He had succeeded in drawing out a number of nobles barricaded in heavily guarded homes, to swell his modest force. Now he had two questions on his mind. Stopping some locals, he asked, "Good sirs, where is the king, and where is the wounded man?"

He was told the king and his soldiers had followed the rebel army northwards, and the wounded man had been taken to St Bartholomew's Hospice and into the care of the nuns. Walworth was still obsessed with seeing Tyler dead, so he sent the bulk of his force after the king, whilst he went to the hospice that bordered the field with half a dozen men. Passing through the open gateway to the brick-walled hospice, Sir William dismounted and marched into the main building and began a search of the patients in their beds.

"I know I have committed murder and will go to Hell, Father, but I did it for my family and for the common man that he might be free of the suffering I've endured." Tyler writhed in agony whilst clutching his leather pouch as a nun tried to mop his brow with a cold, damp cloth. "I regret nothing and die at peace from your blessing, in the hope that I shall soon see my children, but I am sad in the knowledge that my family line ends here. My dying wish is that our rebellion succeeds…"

"Then I shall give you the Last Rites," John Ball replied, leaning over his dying friend. A commotion caught his attention and he turned to see Walworth marching towards them with three men carrying drawn swords, in an all-too-familiar scene from recent history.

"You shall not kill him, in the manner of the slaughter of the saintly Thomas à Becket!" Ball shouted. "This is sacred Church ground!"

"He is no saint, Father," Walworth growled with menace. After a brief scuffle, Ball was pushed aside and a pale and limp Tyler was lifted from his bed, his bloody bandages ripped and hanging loose. A nun screamed, but it did not deter an enraged and obsessed Walworth from dragging his enemy to his followers. "I will give you a traitor's death, Tyler, but not on holy ground. Bring him!"

The rebel leader was dragged from the building and out through the gates to Smithfield where he was forced to kneel on the ground where countless traitors had been executed and livestock slaughtered.

"In the king's name, I brand you a traitor," Walworth growled through clenched teeth, then he lifted his sword and struck Tyler's head from his body. His men cheered as Ball groaned, dropping to his knees, and clasping his hands in prayer. It was over. Walworth was given a short lance to spear Tyler's head on, and he then mounted his horse and set off to find the king.

He found the king, surrounded by his knights, in Clerkenwell fields, still urging the rump of the rebel army to disperse and return to their homes. They would not do so without word of Wat Tyler's fate. Walworth rode to him holding his grisly trophy aloft, eliciting cheers from the king's followers and groans from the commoners.

"It is ended!" Walworth shouted. "Now go home as your king commands!"

A triumphant Walworth saw sadness, weariness, and defeat in the eyes of the peasants, who meekly turned and walked away, with the chirp of crickets in the gloom the final lament on a summer's bloody disquiet.

Burning Shadows

"Two loaves please, Hannah." Ruth reached up to place tuppence on a wooden counter at her eyeline, her friendly smile barely visible to her classmate.

"Oh, got visitors 'ave we?" Hannah replied, placing two freshly baked loaves on the counter.

Ruth narrowed her eyes in recalling her mother's instruction. "Erm, no, just us!"

"Then enjoy, and I'll see you on Monday morning, Ruthie." With that, Hannah wiped the flour on her palms onto her apron and took a step to her left to serve the next customer.

Ruth Swallow left Farriner's Bakery on Pudding Lane, a rectangular loaf under each arm, then cut through a narrow passage to the approach to London Bridge. She glanced to her left, where the bustle of daily life had already begun on the bridge in the pale light of a sun still struggling upwards from the estuary of the river Thames. An upstairs window was flung open on one of the dwellings that lined both sides of the crowded bridge and a woman shook dust from a rug above the heads of those passing beneath.

It was the first day of September 1666, and the long, dry summer was showing no signs of giving way to autumn. Ruth sniffed the warm, still air, hardly noticing the odour of pudding, the offal sold at market, mixed with rotting fish and excrement. Checking to her right and left, she saw a gap between a horse-drawn wagon carrying logs and a smaller hand cart piled with pudding from the meat market, chased by several small, snapping dogs. Safely on the other side, Ruth continued the familiar journey to her home on Saint Bartholomew's Lane.

She daintily swerved the more solid contents of chamber pots that had been emptied onto the cobbles from the upper floors of the townhouses that jutted out over the darkened lane. Early morning movements of workers were generally towards the warehouses on the river, and she hopped out of the way of marching men in hobnail boots on her progress uphill to her mid-terrace home near the top of the lane.

"Here's the bread, Ma!" she cheerfully trilled, then sat on a chair to remove her soiled shoes. "I told a lie to Hannah," she added as her mother's full-length, plain black skirt swept across the stone floor of the kitchen.

Goody Swallow frowned through her wimple at her youngest. "Oh, and what lie did you tell, my fallen angel?" It was a strict Puritan household where prayer meetings were held twice daily around the kitchen table. Falsehoods and blasphemy were considered the unwanted influence of Satan.

"Hannah asked if we had visitors on account of my buying two loaves instead of our usual one," she beamed, thrilled at having transgressed but only on her mother's instructions. "I said, 'no, it's just us'."

At that moment her grandfather entered, scratching at the lice in the thin band of grey between ear and bald pate. "What did I hear about falsehoods being uttered?" he said in a deep, judicial tone. He fixed his gleeful granddaughter with a harsh stare.

"She denied that we had visitors to the baker's girl, is all," good wife Swallow replied, hands on hips.

Goody Swallow's father, William, a learned lawyer who had once held high office during Cromwell's Protectorate, looked down at the girl for a moment, then his round, clean-shaven face cracked in a smile. "Well, my mischievous granddaughter, you are learning the tricks of my profession far too early. You must do penance for knowingly uttering a falsehood, but you also receive my thanks for keeping the secrets of this house that are necessary for us to remain safe in these changing times."

The old man still harboured hopes that the tides of fortune would once again swing back to the Republican cause, as the second King Charles had quickly made himself unpopular with his decadent and debauched ways. That was one reason why William had returned to London from his continental wanderings, another being to visit his daughter's family. He was now using her husband's name of Swallow as his own. Rummaging in his jacket pocket, he produced a farthing, and gave it to the bouncing girl.

Goody Swallow tutted and took her daughter by the hand. "Now, Father, don't be rewarding her for telling lies or she'll learn the wrong lesson." She turned her stern gaze on the grinning girl. "Take that smirk off your face and come with me to the cellar. I'll have you sweeping for the rest of the morning as your penance."

William smiled as his daughter and granddaughter left the kitchen of the wood and mud-panelled terraced house, then fetched a knife to cut a slice off one of the fresh loaves. He spread honey on the bread and added a spoonful to a mug of hot water from a boiling pot on the stove. This was his breakfast, and straight after, he would walk a half mile through the busy streets to the Inner Temple to find the office of an old friend and sympathiser to the cause who shared his profession.

Chewing the last crust, William stood and rinsed his plate and mug in a basin of water. He knew that he had to remain cautious, despite the zeal for hunting down King Charles' killers ebbing away after the mob's subdued reaction to the bloody mutilation of elderly, pious men during the last set of executions. The officers of the King's Privy Council received a clear message that day that it should best be quietly forgotten, and minds turned to other matters, although the new king's thirst for revenge still simmered unabated.

This is what he had heard, but he was well aware there was still a price on his head as one of the last involved in the execution of Charles Stuart who was still unaccounted for. After all, it was his hand that had drafted the execution order. On leaving through the rear door, he tapped a rhythm with his cane on the cobbles, glancing around corners before proceeding.

Later that afternoon, at a wattle and daub lean-to office that backed onto the imposing Guildhall, barely ten minutes' walk from the Swallow residence, a scruffy man knocked on the door of Sir William Hooker, Sheriff of London.

"Enter!" Hooker bawled, and the flimsy wood door creaked open. He groaned at the sight of one of his minions, an ex-royalist corporal named John Davey. "What is it Davey? Can't you see I'm busy?" To demonstrate the point, he spread his hands outwards to unroll a parchment on his desk.

Davey bobbed his head, gripping the brim of his crushed tricorn hat. "Sorry to bother you, Sir William, but will you still be paying the reward of ten pounds for the arrest of one of the notorious regicides who are still at large?" His grin showed blackened gums between his few remaining teeth, causing his master to wince.

"Who is it now?" Hooker asked, exasperated as his underling's obsession. He knew Davey had a gambling addiction that required constant feeding with monies stolen from those he arrested, often on false charges. Davey would take their money and refuse to return it when they were released. He had made many enemies.

"I've been watchin' the Swallow family, sir, and they 'ave been joined by an elderly gentleman who fits the description of William Say. He's the father of missus Swallow, sir, and 'er 'usband is a Puritan minister, Samuel Swallow."

"Damned Puritans! They're responsible for widening the divisions in our land. And damn Cromwell's bones and his bunch of warmongers. They alienated both Catholics and Protestants alike with their over-zealous war on drinking and entertainment, causing great discontent amongst our people …and a loss of trade. All they achieved was isolating England and making us fearful of invasion." He threw a parchment onto his wide and cluttered desk in annoyance.

"They even lined up them fightin' bears against the wall at Tyburn and shot 'em. I saw it with my own eyes, sir. And sent the fightin' dogs to the colonies."

"Well, that may have restricted your gambling options, Davey, but alas, not cured them." He glared at his dirty underling who lowered his eyes and scratched at his groin.

"Shall I apprehend this Master Swallow, sir?" he asked, turning his hat in his calloused fingers. "Then we can question 'im as to 'is being William Say, the villain that took part in the dead king's beheadin'."

Hooker narrowed his eyes and looked down his long nose at the short, scruffy corporal. It had been seventeen years since the king's execution had shocked much of the country and briefly halted a bloody civil war that soon resumed when the equally unpopular Cromwell headed up the Protectorate. After Cromwell's death, this fizzled out and the monarchy was restored in 1660 in the shape of the dead King's son, Charles II, albeit with reduced powers.

A law was passed under the guise of bringing reconciliation, but it also sought to bring those directly involved with the king's execution to justice. That hunt had all but burned out as most had either been executed, assassinated, or died of other causes. But there were still six thought to be alive whose whereabouts remained unknown. "I know a lawyer who was once at the Bar with Say. He could identify him. Yes, bring him in for questioning, but handle him gently, Davey. No roughing him up or tying his hands …or relieving him of his coin. I don't want any more complaints."

Davey backed out of his master's office, bowing and tugging a forelock. He wasted little time in rounding up two thugs and marching on Saint Bartholomew's Lane.

The prayer meeting of ten that included six neighbours broke up at six o'clock, and the kitchen table was repurposed in preparation for the evening meal. Ruth was laying the table when a knock on the door caused the adults to turn to it in apprehension. Goody Swallow peeped through a thick windowpane and smiled to relieve the tension. She opened the door to a grubby youth. "What is it, Thomas?" she enquired.

The boy gripped his cap and answered, "Mistress, it's that man who has been watching your 'ouse who you asked me to keep an eye out for. He's coming down the lane with two others."

"And you shall be rewarded, Thomas," she replied, slamming the door in his face. She turned to the room and announced, "It's the sheriff's man, coming down the lane with two of his thugs. Praise God that my father has not yet returned. Ruthie, run to the alley out the back to keep watch for your grandfather."

The Reverend Swallow placed a comforting hand on his wife's shoulder. "Be calm my dear, sit at the table and be at prayer and I will speak to them."

The group had just taken their seats when there was a loud thump on the door. The Reverend Swallow, a short, thin man dressed in a plain black suit with a starched white shirt collar, opened the door.

The unkempt sight of Corporal Davey stood before him, tapping a cudgel in a dirty palm. "Good day to you, Reverend," he drawled. "I would speak with the old man who 'as been staying here." His sly glint and foul odour caused the godly man to lean back.

"That would be …my father, Master Swallow. His brief visit is over, and he has returned to his village," Swallow replied, saying a silent prayer for his lie.

"Then I am empowered by the Sheriff of London to search this 'ouse for the traitor William Say." With that, Davey barged past the smaller man and entered the kitchen. He surveyed the row of upturned faces around the kitchen table and grunted, seeing no man who had aged sixty summers, and continued to the back living room, then up the narrow staircase to the upper floors.

Goody Swallow ran after him, chiding him for his roughness in casting the candlesticks to the floor. They had no ornaments, so there wasn't much for the ex-soldier to examine. He looked in all the bedrooms, under the beds, and in the cupboards but found no sign of the fugitive, nor any evidence of him having been there. Apart from a locked trunk at the foot of the double bed which the Swallows slept in. "Open it," he ordered.

"I'll fetch the key," she replied, then ran downstairs to her husband. Davey's two thugs were standing in the kitchen, their backs to the door. The prayer group sat at the table, pensive looks on their faces. "Husband, he's asking for the key to the trunk," she whispered.

Reverend Swallow stood and led her back up the stairs, taking a ring of keys from his leather belt on the way. "It's where we keep our best clothes, sir," he said, moving his fingers nimbly along the line of keys. He selected one and knelt to insert it in the lock. At first, he had trouble turning it, eliciting a mischievous grin from their tormentor, whose spittle dripped on the rush mat. Then, with a click, the lock sprang open. Good wife Swallow barely hid a sigh of relief, unaware that she had been holding her breath.

Davey pushed her aside and knelt before the chest. He rummaged through the carefully folded clothes, throwing some out to get to the bottom. There he found half a dozen parchment rolls and some books. "Ah-ha, documents that can stretch a traitor's neck!" he yelled in triumph.

"They are mine, sir. Deeds to this property and others," Reverend Swallow manfully intoned in a pulpit voice that commanded attention. In truth, he hoped the ruffian was illiterate and easily intimidated. "It is an offence against the king's justice to remove such documents from the legal owner without just cause."

Davey hesitated, then narrowed his eyes. "I would take these to my master and 'ave him confirm their exact nature, Reverend," he growled in a low voice.

"Then I must protest…"

But Davey had pushed past him, leaving the books but carrying the six parchment rolls. "They will be returned once Sheriff 'Ooker has seen 'em," he muttered, collecting his two men and leaving through the kitchen door that opened on the lane.

Reverend Swallow briefed and dispersed the group and then turned to his wife. "We must warn your father to stay away from the house. They'll be back once they've read his papers."

Goody Swallow ran to the back door and called for her daughter. "Ruth, my love, I want you to go and find your grandfather, and tell him that the sheriff's men have taken his papers and not to return. We shall pack our things and be ready to move in the morning to our meeting house beyond the Ludgate. Tell him he can find us on the morrow at the Ludgate. Go now, child, and God be with you."

The girl nodded; her eyes still widened from all the excitement.

"Go to the office of his friend, the lawyer Master Rook, you know, where you took a message a month past? You might meet him on the way, so keep your eyes open."

The girl nodded again. She fastened her bonnet, then made her way to the back door to leave down the alleyway, fully understanding the gravity of the situation. Her whole life had been lived in the quiet avoidance of others.

William Say, notorious regicide, was enjoying a glass of port with his old friend, Sebastian Rook, in his cramped office at the Inner Temple, with a view of the square lawn at the centre of the quadrant. His friend lived on the top floor of the three-storey building, as did many working lawyers who spent their days scampering back and forth to the law courts on Fleet Street and The Strand.

"So, my friend, you have lived a life of danger, I hear, keeping one stride ahead of the Royalist mercenaries scouring the continent for their blood money." Leaning back in his armchair, Rook wore a frilled white shirt with a uniform-brown jacket that housed a well-fed belly, and had his greying hair tied back in a ponytail.

Say smiled between sips. "Ah, this is the best port I have tasted in years, my friend. Yes, there was a time of panic when a group of us, living at Vevey in Switzerland under the protection of the Canton's militia, were put on alert by the assassination of our friend and the former chancellor of this land, John Lisle."

Rook shook his head. "Yes, I read he was shot by a blunderbuss in a churchyard in Lausanne by a rogue named MacDonnell." He paused and the men shared a look of sorrow. "Too many learned and God-fearing men have been slain by the vengeful Royalists, although, I can hardly imagine you running, William," Rook added with a smirk.

"Well, they only collected on poor Lisle, as General Ludlow and the rest of us had our guard doubled by our Calvinist friends. I remained there for two more years, then left the lodgings I shared with Cornelius and Andrew, as much out of boredom as anything, and returned to the Netherlands for news. But then we were shocked by the betrayal of Miles Corbet and two others by the turncoat Downing."

"Indeed. It was a bitter business. I saw them hung and quartered at Tyburn. A most distressing sight. But they died well and praised the God of Hosts, shaming the bloodthirsty mob into a subdued silence by the manner of their deaths."

Say put down his empty glass and leaned forward. "The barbarity is on the king's side, alright. His revenge drips with the blood of Godly men."

"Amen to that. But do you believe this year is the end of days, as many of our devout persuasion do, eh, William?" Rook asked.

"I do believe that the second coming of our Lord will be soon, and we shall be with Him in glory on Judgement Day. Perhaps before this year is out, as some of our friends believe. Many perished in last year's plague that some say was the start of it."

"But before then, another glass?" Rook poured for his friend and their reminiscences continued until a clerk interrupted them with a dispatch for Rook. He scanned the document, then said, "I must say farewell, William, for I am summoned to court. Please rest in my quarters for the remainder of the day. I shall convey your legal papers to the relevant authorities once signed. Be assured, your estate will be secured for your wife and children."

"My thanks, Sebastian. I have written to my wife, Anne, requesting her to visit me at her earliest opportunity, and to also sign the papers. I hope it will be soon as I haven't seen her these past six years and look forward to a tender reunion."

"You have sacrificed much, William. Well, good day, and may God protect you."

With that, the two men rose and shook hands. Then William was left alone to see out the hours of daylight, reading a collection of pamphlets on recent events beside a window. He reflected on the words of his friend and offered up a silent prayer that his wife and son were both safe on his estate in Kent. As yet, his assets hadn't been seized by the Crown, and that gave him hope. He was about to close the door of his friend's abode when his granddaughter, Ruth, ran up to him.

"My child, why the haste?" he asked, taking the panting girl by the hand and leading her inside after a furtive glance around the square.

The feisty ten-year-old stopped in the hallway of the stone block building and looked inquisitively at a painting of a castle on the wall. "Grandad, my mama sent me to tell you that you shouldn't come home because some men came looking for you. And they took your papers."

William took off his Dutch cloth cap and unbuttoned his jacket as he guided the girl into the front room. "Sit down, Ruth and tell me what happened in detail."

The following morning, Goody Swallow caught her daughter at the door about to leave for the bakery and held her back by her shoulders. The lane was full of people running in both directions. Looking over the roofs on the opposite side of the lane she saw clouds of black and grey smoke billowing up and only then noticed that the church bells were ringing at an unusual hour. "What's happened?" Goody Swallow called to a neighbour scuttling by.

"'Tis a fire that's burning fierce in Pudding Lane!" the woman shouted on her way past. "They say it started in the bakery!"

Ruth cried out and turned a frightened, pale face to her mother. "I hope Hannah is safe!"

"There, there, Ruthie, I'm sure her father will have taken them all to safety. And now we must do the same. Judging by the smoke, the wind seems to be blowing the fire away from the river." The pensive Puritan good wife looked up and noticed snowflake-like ashes dancing in the breeze.

"There's no way of knowing if this fire will spread or be put out," Reverend Swallow said from behind her. "But we shall not tarry, nonetheless."

The Swallows had already packed their meagre possessions in readiness to flee from the sheriff's men, but now quickened their preparations for a hasty departure. Members of their prayer group had started to assemble outside their house, and soon, everyone was ready to depart Saint Bartholomew's Lane.

They pushed and pulled a cart carrying their combined possessions to the top of the lane, surprised to see so many others fleeing west.

"Ma, the air is so hot and dry that I can hardly breathe!" Ruth gasped.

For the first time, the Swallows could see flames, licking out from the top of Pudding Lane away to their right, greedily snatching the air from the lungs of the terrified populace fleeing before it.

"P'raps 'tis spreading this way after all," Goody Swallow groaned, putting her weight behind a firm push of the cart onto the main road. They turned their backs on the fire and followed the crowd who were funnelling into Lombard Street. Passing the proud mansions of bankers and goldsmiths, they spilled out into the wide square that housed St Paul's Cathedral. The giant building was surrounded by the kiosks of booksellers, who scurried before them with carts piled high with books, maps, and manuscripts. Ruth bent down to pick up a fallen book, looking at the binding and traced the raised golden swirls on the leather cover with her finger. The only book in their house had been a plain black, leather-bound Bible, although her grandfather had some manuscripts and law books in his room. She hid the book under her clothes in her small hand cart.

An explosion coming from the river caused gasps and glances in that direction. "A warehouse has exploded!" a man next to them exclaimed. "'Tis the Dutch - they are storing gunpowder in our city to attack us!" another shouted.

The sound urged the harried Londoners to redouble their efforts to escape the pall of black smoke rising from the glowing inferno barely three streets behind them. The fire was spreading quickly in a pernicious, swirling wind.

Reverend Swallow had removed the tall, black hat that marked him out as a Puritan to wipe the sweat from his brow. "'Tis the end of days as told in the Book of Revelation, in this cursed year bearing the number of the beast, 666."

The stern expressions around him showed this was of little comfort to his group of family and fellow believers. Any further revelations were halted by the splintering of wood accompanied by the groan of collapsing buildings as the insatiable fire ate up the flimsy houses in its path. They felt a rush of hot air on their necks as they picked up their carts and guided them down Ludgate Hill towards the Ludgate - the most westerly gate out of the old medieval walled city.

"We must look for my father amongst the crowd," Goody Swallow shouted above the noise of braying donkeys, honking geese, clucking hens, and the fretful utterances of the fleeing tide of humanity, most of whom had given up their homes and possessions to the greedy flames. A dog snapped at Ruth who cried out in fear, causing her mother to beat the dog away with her staff. The crowd was bunching together as they approached the entrance to the stone gatehouse that was their route to safety.

"Over here!" William Say's firm, commanding voice floated out of the gloom of the gatehouse passage. The Swallows angled their carts towards the damp, brick wall of the ancient archway where William was waiting. He hugged his daughter and granddaughter. "I am much cheered on this miserable day to greet you all," he muttered, shaking his son-in-law's hand.

"Thank the Lord you're safe, William," Reverend Swallow said, reluctant to let go of his hand.

"And thanks to little Ruthie for finding me and warning me off from returning to your house." He pinched the gleeful girl's cheek.

"Aye, but the sheriff's dogs will no doubt be on our trail. Come, let us hurry to my meeting house beyond the Strand." They rejoined the throng moving west, crossing a bridge over the River Fleet that joined the Thames just a hundred yards to their left, then uphill along Fleet Street.

"Did you bring my chest, Samuel?" William asked his son-in-law.

"Aye, but I must tell you that the sheriff's uncouth creature took your rolls of parchment."

"Ah. There's one that will identify me as the man they are searching for. I am sorry to bring danger to you and your family, Samuel." He patted the reverend's back. Both men then leant forward as they doubled their efforts in persuading the family cart uphill.

After a slow procession along the Strand, Reverend Swallow led his group of fifteen or so along a side street on the north side, then onto a narrow lane where the carts had to proceed in single file with two in front and two behind. The lane opened onto a square, where a small Presbyterian brick church with a dirty, white plastered front wall sat next to a wooden barn-like structure occupying one side, flanked by three-storey white and black-beamed townhouses on the three remaining sides. Women scrubbing clothes over basin of dirty water looked up from their doorsteps.

"Here we are," Swallow declared, setting the handles of his cart down and stretching his back. "We agreed some months ago to share a church with a Presbyterian congregation, as their beliefs and practices chime more with our simple faith than that of our proud Anglican brothers. Come, William, let's push our carts to the side door and carry our possessions inside. We'll stay in the loft space above the church. Fear not, for we shall be amongst friends."

Reverend Swallow held a brief discussion with their host, a pale and fretful Presbyterian minister, who guided them up to the loft space above the nave. Already, over thirty congregants had claimed floor space and the new arrivals were allocated one corner of a large area that lacked furnishings or beds.

Their host pointed to a room in the far corner. "That storeroom is the only private space and will be the ablution area. Please draw water from the handpump behind the church and empty your buckets outside each morning. The goodwives shall prepare a communal meal each evening. Also, there's a roof terrace for the hanging of clothes and smoking pipes, should any of the men partake in that fashion."

Goody Swallow's face couldn't hide her anguish at being made homeless. "We shall pray that we're spared having to flee again before the creeping fire."

William squeezed his daughter's hand. "We shall all pray that the fire doesn't spread west of the Ludgate, for the River Fleet forms a natural break. Now, I'll take my granddaughter onto the roof terrace to see what we shall see." He took the tired girl by the hand, and she rewarded him with a thin smile. Outside, they could see westwards over the tightly packed roofs towards the palace at Whitehall where the king resided, and Westminster Hall where parliament met.

"That's where King Charles lives, do you see?" He lifted the girl up and pointed. William also noted that the adjacent warehouse was merely a yard apart, and there was a wide ledge about three feet below his level. With a running jump, he could make it, if the need arose.

"Will the king run away from the fire?" Ruth asked.

"I'd be surprised if he wasn't already upriver at Hampton Court Palace, my dear."

The need for William's escape did arise, some two hours later, when Davey and his men barged their way into the church. It hadn't been difficult for them to pick up the trail of a group of Puritans fleeing west. The Presbyterian minister told them he knew nothing of any traitors and urged them to leave. They barged past him and searched the church, finally confronting Reverend Swallow in the loft. By then, William had gone.

His jump had been successful, and after entering the warehouse through a loft hatch, he climbed slowly and cautiously down from the rafters until he was above a raised platform that he realised was a stage. The building was in use as a playhouse. Below him, two actors were rehearsing their lines. He paused to listen as the shorter of the two gave a speech:

"I am Mosca, a servant, nay a parasite, to a vain master. Your parasite is a most precious thing, dropped from above, not bred 'mongst clods and clotpoles, here on earth. Almost all the wise world is little else, in nature, but parasites..."

The taller of the two men cut a handsome figure, dressed in a frilled shirt and leather hose and boots, occasionally flicking his long, golden locks from a face that bore a cavalier's moustache. The shorter man had the appearance of a domestic servant.

William dropped down onto the stage, startling the two actors, and felt compelled to make a theatrical bow. "Gentlemen, forgive the intrusion. I'm afraid this parasite has dropped on you from above. But I shall not tarry as I am ...being chased by rogues and must flee."

The actors exchanged glances and then the taller man drew a thin-bladed sword and swirled it in William's direction. "Hold, sir. I would enquire as to how you entered our playhouse and from whom are you fleeing?" He took in William's plain mode of dress and added, "And I warrant you're not a patron of the playhouse."

William sighed, and, still catching his breath, replied, "I am no lover of the plays that exalt the baser instincts of Man, 'tis true, but equally, as a lawyer, I am a student of human behaviours and therefore am not opposed to the more insightful studies of our nature. I am no Puritan, sir, and did not delight in the closure of the playhouses."

The actor smiled and made a slight bow, lowering his sword. "Then we are not at odds, sir, particularly when you know that the theme of our play, Ben Jonson's *Volpone*, otherwise known as *The Fox*, is to ridicule the moral corruption of avarice. Not just the love of money but of all objects of human desire."

"'Tis well aimed at our new king," William replied, having recovered his composure.

The actor in the part of Mosca stepped forward with a look of irritation. "This is all well and good, sir, but I would know if the villains chasing you are also under our roof?"

William raised his eyebrows and wondered the same when the main double doors to the building were crudely kicked open and three men stood in silhouette against the odd, orangey glow of the afternoon sun.

"Ah, I would love to discuss the theme of your play further, gentlemen, but it seems my pursuers have found me, and I, like your fox, am cornered by the huntsmen."

Davey and his two thugs marched across the open space towards the stage, swords jangling in scabbards at their sides. "Seize that man!" Davey bawled, pointing at the portly figure of Say. "We're the sheriff's men and 'ave a warrant for 'is arrest."

"Pray, on what charge, sir?" the actor shouted back at Davey, then turned to William and said, "Quick, my friend,

Celia will show you out. We shall keep these crude villains at bay whilst you make good your escape." With that, the actors turned to face Davey and his men, flourishing their swords in a challenge. William turned, noticing a young man dressed as a woman, then exited stage left.

Davey curled back his lips in a gap-toothed grin. "Well, my pretty boys, I would 'ave you know I was a corporal in the king's army and have slain many Roundheads. Step aside so we might apprehend the traitor, William Say, or feel the edge of my sword." The three men moved forward with menace, but the two actors held their ground.

The golden-haired actor swirled his sword and adopted a duellist's stance. "There is the unsavoury whiff of bullyboys about you, and now I recognise you, sir, as the villain who demands taxes from us with threats but has never returned with a permit in the king's name. If you have forgotten to bring proof of payment, then I suggest you return to your lair to get it."

Davey growled and lunged forward, and steel clashed with steel. *Surely, actors only know how to pretend to sword fight?* was the thought in his mind. But the actors parried the thrusts and slashes of the sheriff's men with skill and speed, then counter-attacked with well-aimed blows that touched, but barely pricked their foes' clothing.

Mosca, short but stocky, made the point. "To make a convincing sword fight on stage, we must know our craft." With that, he lunged forward, deftly removing a button from one of the brutes' jerkin with a flick of his sword.

His fellow actor laughed and added, "We practice many hours so that our fights are realistic and we have the skill to not cut each other." He attempted the same, but Davey dodged his blade. "Our swords are real, gentlemen, not wooden like those of a child."

After another parry and thrust, Davey shouted, "This has gone on long enough!" He tried to barge past his tormentor with a cry of rage, "Do not come between the sheriff's men and…"

Davey didn't finish his sentence as the taller actor stepped to one side and tripped him as he rushed past, sending him sprawling across the stage.

The actors exchanged glances and the golden cavalier held his hands up in an act of surrender, thinking they had bought the fugitive lawyer enough time to make good his escape. "Gentlemen, I apologise for delaying you, and thank you for the sparring lesson. And please return soon with our permit."

"I'll be back for you, alright," Davey growled as he got to his feet and led his men into the dark wing of the stage, groping around for a way to the wall. From there, they moved along the side of the wooden building until they found the rear door and exited into the mad, orange glow of a fire-lit sky.

William was led through narrow passages until his guide stopped and pointed to a movement of people on a busy street. "The Strand, sir. I advise you to cross over and make your way to the river and take a ferry to Southwark. Good luck to you." With a swish of his skirt, he turned and walked away.

"My thanks, fair Celia!" William shouted after him, then turned and hurried to find sanctuary amongst the fearful throng. He jostled against the flow of humanity towards the fire into Fleet Street, then down an alleyway to the Temple to look for his friend. To his relief, he found Sebastian Rook in the throes of giving instruction to a group of men in carrying his trunks of personal effects and books towards the river.

"Ah, William! I am taking a boat to Richmond and my summer residence. Will you join me? The fire is consuming St Paul's Cathedral and will soon be at the Ludgate."

He pointed between a gap in the buildings and the puffing William, hands on knees, saw yellow and orange flames licking around the pointed spire of the tallest building in England. He let out a groan but couldn't speak as he was still gulping air into his heaving lungs. Sebastian's grim expression was fixed as he guided his friend to sit on his doorstep. "Catch your breath, William. I fear those who predicted the end of our world this year may have a point. I shall fetch you a cup of water."

Half an hour later, they were on the raised deck of an elongated skiff with six oarsmen on each side. A family begged for deliverance, but Rook shook his head and ordered his men to cast off.

"I am relieved to be on the river, my friend, as the sheriff's men nearly had me at the meeting house," Say explained whilst scanning the shore for sight of his pursuers. "I have also learned that you can find friends in the most unexpected of places."

"Then it's God's will that you are saved, William. To hunt you still for your part in Cromwell's obsession is unjust, in my view. The Indemnity and Oblivion Act was intended to bring reconciliation and put the past to bed, but the new king used it only to pursue his vengeance. I warrant we'll be safe at Richmond."

"Aye. My thanks again, Sebastian. My old bones cannot take much more of this. But we must spend our time in prayer to the Lord of Hosts to ready our souls for a sterner judgement." The sight before them was one never to be forgotten, for however many days that remained of the world of Men. The river was a bustle of boats, mainly ferries taking distressed families from the north bank to the south, whilst the sight of St Paul's burning brightly beneath a sombre, darkened sky, framed a scene of utter devastation. Warehouses along the river burnt fiercely, as did the first three houses on London Bridge in the distance. A warehouse exploded, sending white and blue sparks mixed with yellow high over the river in an unnatural rage, causing a wherry to capsize and the two friends to shudder.

"This has the whiff of God's judgement, alright," Rook muttered, gripping the rail as the boat rocked in a gentle swell.

William's feet were planted wide apart, as he had learned from his Channel crossings. He linked his plump fingers in the act of prayer. "May God our Father watch over my daughter and her family, until such a time as they meet our maker on Judgement Day, whether this be it, or it is yet to be."

The birds had fled the skies and the only sound was that of oars splashing in the opaque, brown flow of the river as the skiff moved upstream. They rounded a bend so that all that could be seen on the horizon was a column of black smoke rising to the heavens.

"There is meaning in this, but what is the lesson?" Rook asked.

"Either a divine rebuke, the wicked tongue of Satan, or the opening act of Doomsday?" William's thoughts turned to little Ruth and a tear welled.

"An eye for an eye, 'til we're all blinded," he muttered, wiping his face with a kerchief.

"What's that, William?" Rook enquired.

"If I gave myself up to the king's justice, would his revenge be satisfied, and my family be saved from persecution?"

"The king would have your head on a spike, but his thirst for revenge will not be slaked until the last of you is dead," Rook replied. "This is a man who had Cromwell's body dug up to display his rotting head on a pole. He would soon find another cause for his vengeful spirit to feast on. Do not doubt the importance of removing his father, the tyrant Charles Stuart, William, and ending the age of absolute monarchy. We shall bide our time, whatever time there is, and if the world doesn't end, then we shall be here to curb the excesses of this arrogant, restored king. Parliament will rise again."

William nodded at his friend's soothing words, but his eyes remained fixed on the foul, black spew issuing from Satan's gaping maw. All was not well in the world of Men; on that, all could agree.

Holly's Dream

The face of a young girl stares up at me from under the ice on the frozen river. Her eyes are wide with fear and pleading - the palms of her small hands pressing upwards on the unyielding ice. She mouths the word, "Help!" in a stream of bubbles. I look around frantically for help, from an adult, perhaps - anyone older than my fourteen years.

"Hey, Mister!" I cry to a gent in a top hat skating nearby. He skates towards me and sees the form of the girl, her brown woollen coat buttoned with wooden pegs, moving slowly downstream under the ice. He moves ahead of her with well-practiced swishes of his skates, his coattails swinging behind, towards a group of fishermen whose lines are dangling through neatly cut holes in the ice. He shouts a command at them, and they doff their caps in subservience. I follow, mimicking his skating motion on my boots wrapped in cloth rags.

He chooses a hole that is in line with her motion, instructs a man to pull up his fishing line, then takes off his coat, rolls up his sleeves, drops to his knees and holds his arm under the freezing water, reaching for the girl. He grabs her coat lapel and pulls her up through the hole, to the cheers of the ragged fishermen. I look down on her unmoving, rigid body, held in his arms like a rag doll, her bonnet askew, eyes closed, lank brown locks like river weed, skin blue and wrinkled…

*****

This is my recurring dream - or nightmare, if you will. I always wake in a state of anxiety straight after, not knowing the fate of the girl. I've decided to follow my papa's advice. He says it's my imagination still working after I've gone to sleep, allied to a primal fear of drowning. We had gone to the frost fair on the frozen River Thames a few weeks before, to celebrate the Iron Duke's victory over Napoleon in the latest of the Spanish Wars in this year, 1814. I slipped and fell onto the hard ice and kept tight hold of papa's hand after that. Since Mama died of the coughing sickness, I've become closer to my papa.

That night I'd woken him with my first nightmare. He tucked me back up in bed with soothing words and proposed that I exorcised these ghostly images by writing the rest of the story as I imagine it, giving it a proper, and satisfying, ending. Well, it's worth a try, so here's my story, made up with my own ideas and scraps I got from my chambermaid, Mabel.

*****

She splutters and retches, choking up the river water - she's alive!

I stand close by and slyly relieve the concerned gent of his pocket watch - for that is my business - and I tell him that I'll look after the girl, pretending to know her, then I led her away through the bustle of the market stalls of the frost fair.

My name is Holly and I live in a terraced townhouse house in Southwark, south of the river, in this reign of Mad King George, with my mam and three sisters. Papa died last year from consumption, his thin frame wracked with coughing fits until his wheezy breath slowed to a rattle, then stopped, like the mantlepiece clock when it hadn't been wound up. Now I help out by stealing what I can with my gang.

I don't want to be a thief, but needs must. We call ourselves "The Collectors", and we take what we lift to a long-bearded Jew in Whitechapel who gives us pennies and occasionally sixpences for our haul. I give most of my share to Mam, telling her I've found work sewing for a lady. I keep a few pennies for myself in a leather pouch in a hole in my mattress. Maybe one day I'll have enough to go to a proper school and learn to be a seamstress.

"Here, girl! Come here," a man shouts at me as I make my way up Farringdon Lane, heading towards the fish market. I don't know him, maybe he's someone I've robbed before. I start to walk briskly away, ignoring his calls, but he persists and follows me. People are starting to look at us.

"I don't mean to hurt you," he calls, as he tries to catch up with me. "I'm from the Cardus Home for Orphans." Now I'm curious and I slow so he can catch me up. "Child," he puffs, "I believe you're the one who helped rescue a girl from under the ice?"

"Yes, sir," I reply, managing a half-curtsey. "I helped that poor girl out of the river. She was half-drowned and freezing cold. She was taken away by some fine people who said they would see to her. But how did you know it was me that helped her?"

"Well, she was brought to my house by a gentleman who gave me your description - I've been on the lookout for a …street girl with long, reddish hair since then. My name is Donald Albright, and I'm the director of a reputable home for orphaned girls. You may have heard of us, the Cardus Home?" He removed his top hat and bowed to me. That had never happened before, and I let out a giggle at his fine manners.

"No sir, I haven't. I'm just an 'umble girl from the East End, that's all I can tell you, sir. I just 'appened to be on hand to help that girl. Is she alright?"

"Oh yes, dear child, she has recovered and she's asking if she can meet those who helped her. Can I take you to meet her, so she can thank you?"

"Well, I'm supposed to be buying fish for my mam, sir."

"I can arrange for you to return home in a carriage and stop at the market with a few pennies from my pocket for your fish, and a few vegetables for your table. May I ask your name?"

"My name's Holly Fanshaw, sir, from Whitechapel."

"Well, Holly, will you come with me?"

He walks me to his carriage and his footman holds the door open for us. We ride in the carriage, and I see London in a different light - looking over the heads of the ordinary folk at the fine buildings, with their ornate gas lamps and brightly coloured curtains and drapes. I see Westminster Abbey and the devilish gargoyles looking down as we head west, and finally stop in a street in Chelsea outside the orphanage building. My wanderings have taken me here as it's close to the meat market - a good place to lift wallets and watches.

"Follow me, Holly, there's someone who'll be happy to meet you," he says, helping me down from the carriage by my hand as if I'm a lady. There's a matron holding the door open, and we enter a large hallway. I'm guided towards a door that opens into a salon with fine chairs and paintings on the wall.

A girl stands up to greet me, and I recognise the pretty face of the girl from under the ice. She has red ribbons in her light brown curls. She runs towards me and hugs me as if I'm her long-lost sister. Her name is Mabel, and we sit and chatter. I tell her that she looks much better with the colour back in her rosy cheeks. She tells me she was running across the bridge, trying to escape from bad people who tried to kidnap her, and tumbled over the edge, falling onto the ice, cracking it, and slipping underneath. That's when she saw my face on the other side as she was desperately struggling to find a way to get out.

"I wanted to thank you, and invite you to live here with us," she says, just like that, with wide, blue eyes. She keeps glancing at Mr Albright. There's something else. Uncertainty or fear.

"I live with my family, miss, in Whitechapel," I reply. She looks all sad and starts to cry. The gentleman, Mr Albright, comes over and puts a hand on my shoulder.

"I was hoping you'd say yes to our invitation, Holly. You see, we gather up the poor children from the streets and find them nice homes to live in. We give them an education so they can become productive members of society." He smiles at me, and I shake free of his grip.

"I'd like to get an education, sir, that's true, but I ain't leaving my mam and sisters. I'm the eldest and they need me," I say, standing up and backing towards the door as I start to feel uncomfortable. The big matron in her blue uniform and white apron is waiting by the door and grabs me firmly with both hands.

"You'll do what Master Albright says, my girl," she says, and marches me up the stairs to a room at the top of the house where I'm shoved in and the door locked behind me. It's an attic that runs the length of the house, with rows of bunk beds on either side of a narrow passage. Now I understand who Mabel was running away from. This place is like a prison for poor girls - and now I'm one of them.

Over the next few days, I'm forced to wear a uniform and muck in with the other girls. There are about thirty of us, ranging in age from six to fifteen. Alice, or Matron Malice as the girls call her, slaps or pinches anyone who steps out of line. We are fed thin gruel and taught how to sew and clean a room, in preparation for being sold to fine folk as housemaids. I've seen money handed over to Mr Albright by ladies and gents who then take one of the girls away.

After a few weeks, I make an escape plan. Mabel is the only one I trust, and she says she wants to come with me. Also, she managed to get outside once before… although she ended up in the river. I wonder if she was pushed over the bridge railings, as it's difficult for short people to fall over them. She says she doesn't know as it all happened so quickly. Well, I think we can expect to be killed or sold as slaves if they catch us, so we'd better make a good job of it, I tell her.

In the back garden there's a workhouse; a long, wooden shack where us girls sit on benches either side of a long table and sew or knit dresses and scarves until our fingers bleed. The building has a flat roof, I notice, and I see there's a gap no wider than my height from a ledge beneath a first-floor window to the roof of the workhouse. The wide ledge runs around the side of the building. There's a ladder fixed to the brickwork from this first-floor ledge up to the window on the third-floor landing. Escape is on my mind.

The weather changes and it becomes less cold. From our attic I can hear the ice on the river cracking, and from the small window I see ice blocks moving downriver in white chunks, glimpsed between buildings in the orange glow of the sunset. The icicles melt and fall from the eves and I tell Mabel we'll go that night. There's a ledge outside our window that leads to the back of the house where Mabel says there's an iron ladder in case there's a fire.

Matron does her rounds to make sure we're all in our wooden cots and blows out our candles. An hour or so later, by the light of a full moon, we get dressed, just the two of us. The other girls, tired out, sleep soundly, the gentle rhythm of their breathing is a comfort to me as I pull on some woollen stockings. I take Mabel's hand and lead her out to the landing. I pause as a floorboard creaks, then we continue in the silence of the sleeping house.

We creep to the window at the end of the corridor. There, we gently raise the sash window and I climb out into the cool night air, then hold it open for Mabel. Moonlight illuminates the top of the iron ladder. Down we go, past two sets of windows, to the ledge that leads us to the back garden, and onto the flat roof of the workshop. I lower myself onto a water butt and help Mabel. The garden is walled and the gate is padlocked. We quietly move a bird table against the wall and climb up and over, dropping down into a dark alleyway. I hold her hand and we edge along until my foot hits something - a homeless man, who wakes and curses me, pulling a torn blanket from under my foot. We run to the light at the end of the alleyway, out into the street, and towards freedom.

The moon disappears behind the clouds, but the street is lit by gas lanterns on high poles. I've rarely walked around after midnight, so find these new gas lamps to be the most wondrous things, and I glance up at the flickering flames. We head east, past Westminster Abbey, following the line of the river. Night watchmen hunch over their brazier, warming their hands. One turns to stare at us as we hurry past, but says nothing. After a while, I turn at the sound of horse hooves on the cobbles, and gasp at the sight of Master Albright's footman on his Hanson carriage, swishing his whip over the horse's rump.

"Quick, this way!" I hiss, in a loud whisper, grabbing Mabel's hand and running down a narrow passageway between two warehouses towards the river.

We run along the embankment and onto Old London Bridge, its leaning houses lit by the eerie glow of gaslights. There are lights from the windows, as some foolhardy folk still stubbornly live in the structures condemned for demolition. To cheer us up, I start singing in puffs of cloudy breath:

London Bridge is falling down,
Falling down, falling down.
London Bridge is falling down,
My fair lady.

Mabel smiles and sings the next bit, as we swing our arms:

Build it up with wood and clay,
Wood and clay, wood and clay,
Build it up with wood and clay,
My fair lady.

"It'll take much more than wood and clay to fix this bridge," I say, stopping to look back. The bridge approach is shrouded in darkness, and all is still.

I lead Mabel between houses to the railings to catch our breath and I look down on the river. The edges are still solid ice with people on. Ice flows to my left are like an army of snow dwarves bobbing down the dark central channel. I study the pinpoints of light where coals glow red in braziers as groups huddle around, warming their hands or toasting bits of meat on skewers. I'm transfixed in that moment and feel myself frozen to the spot. A squeeze on my hand brings me to my senses.

"They should be careful," Mabel says in cloudy puffs, "that ice will be thinning." There is fear in her eyes at a returning memory, and I hug her.

A girl screams, and a shudder runs through me, but it's only a redcoat soldier, grabbing a girl who struggles playfully. She breaks away from his grasp and shuffles across the ice in shoes wrapped in rags, glancing back, hoping he will follow. He does and grabs her arm by the steps that go to the embankment walk.

A cold wind pinches my face and I brush a strand of red hair away with my mitten. Jeers and laughter rise up from the last remnants of the frost fayre, as I pull Mabel's hand and return to the main road across the bridge. I notice wooden panels and lumps of plaster around my feet, a sign of the danger from falling masonry. I smile at a memory from a few months ago when one of my gang had been hit on the head by a thin square of wood. He wasn't badly hurt, and we had laughed at his misfortune.

"Oi, stop!" The voice of the footman floats out of the gathering fog, as his carriage clatters onto the bridge. Mabel points and gasps, and we turn and run to the other side, disappearing into the dark, rabbit warren of streets in Southwark to hide in a doorway. We stay hidden until the carriage clatters by.

"I know of a tavern where some older boys hang about," I whisper and lead the way there. Despite the lateness of the hour, I find three youths clustered around a brazier, toasting chestnuts. One of them is Thomas, a friend and fellow thief, who welcomes me with a hug. I quickly explain that we've escaped from enforced servitude and are being pursued. The boys are ripe for mischief, and they tell me to make my way home whilst they see off the carriage by throwing stones at the horse so the driver whips him away.

With a laugh, we run for home, fingering the warm, round chestnuts in our pockets that Thomas gave us. No one's under the ice, just the fish and Old Father Thames, and we've made good our escape.

There's no one about and we follow a trail of gas lights along a main road until we turn off into the darkness towards my row of three-storey tenements. Stopping to catch our breath, I look down into Mabel's blue, pleading eyes. She has nowhere to go.

"You'll come home with me," I say, taking her hand. "We've seen the back of Matron Malice and Master Albright, and can now do as we please." We crunch through frozen snow in the pre-dawn gloom, stepping over hardened lumps of horse manure. The upper floors are shrouded in a low-hanging fog that hovers over us. We're now wiser to the tricks of ensnarement and glad of the prospect of a lumpy, straw-stuffed sack as a mattress.

"This is it, Mabel. We're home at last."

*****

I'm in my room at my sunlit desk, dipping my nib in an inkwell, hurriedly scrawling the end of my story. Once the final line is written, I lean back with a sense of satisfaction, then gently blot the page. It has taken me two days to write my account. I gather up my pages and go in search of Papa.

I find him smoking his pipe and reading a newspaper in the drawing room, and I announce that I've finished my story.

"That's wonderful, Holly. Now read it to me so I can know the fate of the girl under the ice."

I clear my throat and read slowly, deliberately, enunciating my words clearly as I've been taught by my English tutor. I finish telling my story and smile at Papa, but he has a stern look, and I fear he's about to rebuke me.

"Holly, it's a fine tale that shows a talent for storytelling," he says, but then he tuts. "But I'm most aggrieved that you identify with a common thief. You have everything you need here, and I hope that you're not tempted to lift things that aren't yours. I would hope that Mabel wouldn't become a street thief and both girls would earn an honest living as a seamstress, as they were taught during their period of captivity. London is full of thieves, and I would be sorely aggrieved if my daughter joined their ranks!"

I run to him and hug him tight. "Oh Papa! It's just a story, part of which I heard from Mabel, our chambermaid, who I questioned closely for ideas. I would never let you down with such wicked behaviour. I shall add on a final paragraph to say the girls became the most skilled and highly sought after seamstresses in Southwark, and in time found honest men to marry."

He smiled and stroked my hair. "Then I hope your thrilling tale with its happy ending has diverted your mind away from your nightmare of slipping under the ice. The great thaw has begun, and we can look forward to warmer days. Come, let's go find a street seller for some hot chestnuts. Your story has given me an appetite."

"Will London Bridge fall down, Papa?" I ask.

"It'll be demolished soon and they've already set the foundations next to it for a new bridge, my dear," he replies. "The evidence of progress is happening all around us."

I wrap my shawl around my shoulders and take his arm. I'm almost as tall as my dear departed mama, and I resolve to be a support to my downcast, unhappy papa. A passing officer twisting his long whiskers gives me a wink as he lifts his pointed hat. Wellington's victories have lifted our spirits, and I skip towards the chestnut seller's brazier, turning to smile at Papa. I am Holly, writing my own story. In time, I shall be a wife and mother, and mistress of a fine townhouse in this wondrous time of mad King George.

Cherry Blossoms Fall

The all clear sounded like Mother's loving call to sweet, milky tea with bread and jam. I followed the eyebrow pencil lines drawn on the calves of a matronly figure up the circular stairwell of High Street Kensington Underground Station towards welcoming shafts of sunlight. It was Spring, 1941, and my celebratory mood at my recent appointment as a junior doctor at the Charing Cross Hospital Mortuary had been tempered by the anxiety of life in London during The Blitz. German bombing raids had certainly upped the number of fatalities in the terror-stricken city, leading to my opportunistic appointment after graduating from medical school. 'We must do what we can to help the War effort, Doctor Robinson', I'd been told at my job interview, but for now, I was meeting a friend and fellow graduate for lunch.

A foot-wide stream ran along the gutter, spurting water from the bent thumb of a bomb-damaged hydrant that caused delight in children but groans from their fussing parents. Daylight bombing raids were unusual, as Fritz preferred to come over under the cover of darkness. The Blitz had now dragged on for nine, nerve-shredding months of punishment and random deaths; London had become a patchwork quilt of rubble mountains in vacant plots.

"Oh, a wall has collapsed onto the lovely garden!" the matronly figure exclaimed.

I followed the direction of her mortified gaze to a square patch of grass bordered by an array of different trees; its lawn and flower beds now discoloured by a layer of dust that had crept outwards from a bomb-damaged apartment block. The entire front wall of the building had fallen in an untidy heap of shattered red bricks across an access road and spilled onto the communal garden where a forlorn tree trunk denuded of branches poked out of the mess of masonry and household items. The rooms in the once-private four-storey residence were now exposed for all to see, like an abandoned dolls house. Privacy was just one lost innocence to the brutality of war.

Black-uniformed air raid wardens were corralling the public away from the mess, occasionally blowing their whistles to assert their authority.

"Excuse me," I said, grabbing one by his sleeve.

He looked me up and down, no doubt assessing my social status before choosing his level of response. He saw a clean-shaven young man six inches taller than him, dressed in a crumpled grey suit, off-white shirt, old school tie, black brogues and a dark grey trilby hat.

"No need to grab me, sir. How can I help?"

"I think I can see a body lying on the floor of the first-floor room over there." I pointed to one of the rooms in the derelict doll's house. A lump shaped like the curved profile of a woman in a dark dress lay on the tattered remains of a carpet close to the edge of the cavity.

He peered through narrowed eyes, most likely seeing little more than a blurred landscape. "I'll look into it, sir. You can go about your business."

"Well, I am a doctor, so I think I'd better wait here for you to bring the body down, in case the victim is still alive." I smiled but maintained a fixed posture of authority.

He narrowed his eyes again, drew his whistle, and blew two short-tempered blasts. On hearing their summons, two young men with Red Cross armbands appeared with a stretcher from the back of a stationary ambulance. The warden pointed to the building and shouted, "Body on the first floor." He grunted at me and wandered off, revealing, like a prop on a stage, a cherry blossom tree in bloom next to the pile of rubble. It's pretty, serene, pink and white blossoms seemed out of place in the scene of destruction, the petals defiled by grey masonry dust in an unhappy union. In that moment I understood the extent to which our cosy world had been shattered, beauty desecrated by brutality, perhaps forever. Was this merely the overture to an opera of hate and wanton destruction? A retelling of the Great War but with an enhanced destructive power?

I pulled down the brim of my trilby, crossed the road, and lit a Marlboro cigarette from a soft pack I'd been given by a grateful GI whose troublesome appendix I had recommended he get looked at. Glancing down, I noted that mud had splattered on my trouser leg and polished brogues in the dash across the road. The scent of the petrol fumes off the lighter coupled with the draw of tobacco were a comforter in times of stress, and there were plenty of those in a typical day in wartime London. I checked my watch. 12.30. Still time to make my lunch appointment in a nearby pub.

"Got the time, sir?"

I turned to my left to a man in a dark blue greatcoat, but with stubble on his chin and overgrown, uncombed black hair that sprouted from his head like unruly weeds, matched by thick eyebrows above black, roving eyes. A serviceman on leave, perhaps?

"Yes, it's just gone 12.30."

He rocked from one foot to another, as if there was more. "Shocking, that. I know people who live in that block. Or lived, I should've said."

"Oh, I hope they're all right," I replied.

He tried a grin. "This war's a time of great danger and loss, all right," he replied, stating the obvious.

"Ah, they're bringing out a woman on that stretcher. I'd better get back over there to check on her. Good day." I glanced back at the man as I crossed the road. His eyes followed me as he scratched his head. Lice or agitation? Anxiety had become a feature of this damned war.

Stretcher bearers were making a beeline for the ambulance.

"Can you stop, please? I'm a doctor." They duly complied and I saw they had covered the unmoving form with a grey blanket. A gentle gust of wind blew a handful of cherry blossoms onto her; nature's last rites. I carefully lifted back the blanket and examined her. "Hmm. She's had a nasty bang on the back of the head. Perhaps she fell against an item of furniture?" A patch of congealed blood matted her hair.

"She was curled up behind a sofa, sir. No sideboard or other furniture near her, unless it fell out when the wall came daahn," one of the orderlies drawled.

I eyed the pock-marked youth and had a quick look at the rest of her. No other signs of trauma, just the bang on the head, although I had no way of knowing if any bones were fractured. I tilted her head towards me and saw what looked like red finger marks on her alabaster neck, and noted the dark rings around her puffy, blood-shot eyes on an otherwise serene face. I gently closed her eye lids. She was an attractive, well-groomed woman in her mid-thirties, I estimated, in a cotton dress with white frills at the collar and cuffs. Had she tailored it herself? One of her shoes was missing. She had real stockings, not the drawn-on pretence. A quick check of her hands showed broken and bloody fingernails. Any jewellery she may have been wearing was missing, with a tell-tale white mark where a wedding ring once sat.

"Please take her to Charing Cross Hospital mortuary. Tell them Doctor Robinson sent you with a suspicious death. I'll examine her there." I covered her with the blanket and stepped back. I would have loved to have searched the pockets of the orderlies, but such an accusation would have caused a scene. Besides, I didn't have the authority to do so.

"Funny thing, sir. She's the third woman we've removed from a bomb site who looks like she's been knocked abaaht a bit. But I admit, it's difficult to tell which injuries 'ave or 'aven't been caused by the bombings…"

"Alright, Alfie," his mate interjected, "let's not keep the nice gentleman."

With that, they hurried off to the ambulance. I followed to the corner of the square and looked up and down the road. The man in the navy greatcoat had gone. Why was I looking for him? I continued on my way along Kensington High Street for three blocks, then rounded a corner to see a familiar pub sign, The Prince of Wales.

Through a blue-grey haze, I found the booth where my friend Alice from medical school sat behind a glass of port and an overflowing ashtray. We were medical school study mates in our mid-twenties, now in junior doctor posts at different hospitals. "Sorry I'm late. Had to duck into The Underground when the air raid siren sounded."

"I forgive you," she replied, putting me at ease with a welcoming smile. "I also scurried into the communal air raid shelter on Cromwell Road."

"A death trap if it took a direct hit. Another drink?"

"Always. Port, and a bully beef sandwich, if there's any going."

I took off my suit jacket and a solitary white blossom fluttered from the shoulder onto the table.

"Ah, *Prunus Umineko,* otherwise known as the Japanese Cherry Blossom Tree," Alice said, turning it over in her hand, admiring the pink cluster surrounded by eight white petals. "May I keep this? I'll press it and add it to my collection. But before that, I'll wear it on my walk back to work."

Not waiting for my answer, she worked the flower over her left ear, kept in place by her luxuriant golden curls. Her strawberry-blonde locks turned golden in direct sunlight, transforming her into a goddess. Britannia's peace-loving sister, ready to heal and comfort the wounded.

"Of course. A perfect pairing of beauty in an otherwise grey and downbeat landscape. Your horticultural expertise is once more exalted, dear Alice. It came from a shocked cherry tree beside a collapsed wall."

"Then I think I know where you were. A lovely little handkerchief of green space wedged between The Underground and a row of apartment blocks. I've sat on the bench beneath that pretty tree. Everything gets spoiled eventually in this awful war."

I returned five minutes later carrying a circular bar tray with drinks and a plate on which sat a single, large sandwich made of thick white bread, cut from corner to corner. "It's a generously carved bread doorstep crammed with bully beef and sliced tomatoes. I thought we could share?"

She smiled sweetly, then contorted her face and crossed her blue eyes as she attacked the sandwich, in a parody of a recent Marx Brothers film we'd seen. Her almost-white eyelashes and brows were practically invisible on her pale face. She didn't wear makeup on work days. I smiled at her golden curls bouncing in the attack on the super-sized sandwich.

We chewed and sipped in silence, enjoying the simple things that made the deprivations of war bearable. Our mornings started at eight o'clock, so by one, we'd worked up appetites that even cataloguing the grisliest cadavers couldn't diminish. In the midst of death, life goes on.

I polished off my half of the sandwich and washed it down with a half pint of ale, smacking my lips in satisfaction. "I've just examined the body of a woman carried from a bombed building."

"Why on earth did you do that?"

"A hunch. A wall had collapsed to reveal a number of rooms, and I saw her lying in the ruins of her lounge. I sent stretcher bearers to bring her body down. She was dead. I gave her a superficial examination and noted a blunt trauma wound on the back of her head. Her hair was matted with congealed blood. Like it hadn't just happened during the air raid, but some time before."

Alice switched to her serious doctor's face, pursing her lips. "There are whispers amongst the porters that you could get away with murder during the blackouts. Us women are particularly vulnerable. The few police who've avoided conscription or been diverted to other duties have their hands full with The Blitz. I bet there's very few murders being investigated."

"There was an odd chap in a navy greatcoat hanging about. He asked me the time and seemed agitated. It all left me feeling rather unnerved."

Alice's shrill laugh made others look. I noted their smiling faces. A moment of levity that had lifted some out of their sombre moods. "You really are channelling your inner Sherlock Holmes, Martin. Don't look now, but I think he's standing at the bar."

I looked at her, trying to decide if she was serious or just pulling my leg. She kept smiling and nodded her head slightly towards the bar. I dropped my napkin and when picking it up, I glanced behind me at the bar counter. Half a dozen men were standing there, some reading newspapers laid out on the wide oak counter. At the far end, a man in a navy coat was raising a half pint glass of stout to his lips, facing the bar, his shaggy, unkempt hair at odds with the other neatly trimmed customers and bar staff. We made brief eye contact in the bar mirror. My heart skipped a beat as I sat up rigidly. "It's him."

"Well, I think I could give a description of him if you fail to make it back to work. Let's go. I'll escort you to the end of the road. That's the best I can do, I'm afraid. But keep me informed of what you find out from your examination of the dead woman. I'm intrigued."

With that, we finished up and left, walking to a T-junction where our ways parted. I could see the tower turrets of Charing Cross Hospital, barely four hundred yards in the distance. Looking back, there was no sign of the man.

"Well, cheerio, dearest. I'll call you later this evening at your digs. About nine. The anxiety of the air raids is definitely getting to me."

I kissed her cheek and caught a fragrant whiff from the blossom in her hair. My left hand instinctively slid into my jacket pocket, fingering a velvet ring pouch my mother had given me, hope for love glistening in her eyes. "It was your grandmother's," she'd told me.

I turned and strode purposefully towards the river. Glancing up at the blue sky contained between the walls of warehouses, I marvelled at the wormcast vapour trails made by the engines of German bombers and RAF fighters locked in a life-or-death battle above the indifferent flow of the timeless River Thames. A mechanical leap forward from a bygone age when ancient man cowering from a comet and inventing a story of a dragon flying across the sky to earn an extra portion around the campfire that evening.

*****

The mortuary at Charing Cross Hospital occupied the basement of the Victorian-era building, with austere red floor and wall tiles, perhaps chosen to hide any drips or dissected organ pieces that fell to the floor. Above the tile line, plastered brick walls were painted silky cream, and the high windows, evocative of a prison, let in some daylight from the street level.

Corpses were stored in refrigerated drawers along two walls, and new arrivals lay covered in sheets on trolleys, awaiting their turn to be examined by a doctor to establish the cause of death. A clerk would then seek to identify them, usually from identity cards, rent books, or work-related documents, then find the next of kin and arrange for the body to be released for burial. "Unknowns" and those without any family were assigned for mass burial. The third, much smaller category, was "suspicious deaths" for the attention of the coroner. We soon became inundated with bodies after the Luftwaffe's bombings started in September 1940, and experienced sharp spikes in admissions after each air raid.

My immediate superior was Doctor Clement Bow, the head of the mortuary, a frail, balding man in his late sixties, whose retirement was delayed in 1939 after emergency measures were introduced at the start of the war. I was one of the three junior doctors on his team, and our main concern was to leave him to the quiet sanctuary of his office unless something out of the ordinary happened.

I rapped on the frosted window of his door and pushed it open. "Doctor Bow?"

He looked up from the report on his desk and regarded me over the top of his spectacles. "Ah, young Robinson. Come in."

"Sorry to bother you, but there's a new arrival, a woman, who I think could be a suspicious death."

"Oh? And what makes you think that?"

"Well, I saw a body being removed from a bomb site on Kensington High Street, and my instincts drove me to make a cursory examination of the deceased woman. There are signs of violence, sir."

"Do you often intercept stretcher bearers on your lunch break, Robinson?" he tetchily replied. He hated being dragged from his swivel chair. He also hated summoning the coroner, Professor Simpson, whose haughty manner led us all to stand to attention and jump into action at his slightest command. "Lead on, young Robinson. Let me examine the unfortunate woman."

Fifteen minutes later, Doctor Bow agreed with my initial prognosis and visibly sighed after instructing one of the clerks to get Professor Simpson on the telephone. Turning to me, he said, "do you recall the case a few months ago, Doctor Robinson, of the professor's expert testimony at the High Court that convicted an odious criminal dubbed "the Blackout Ripper" by the press?"

"I do indeed, sir. Professor Simpson is credited with devising a facial reconstruction technique using an X-ray overlaid onto a photograph to identify one of the victims. Other evidence from the post-mortem tied the victims to their murderer. Quite remarkable, and whilst all these German bombs were falling about us…"

"Quite so. But because of his newfound celebrity status, I'm concerned he'll turn our mortuary into a media circus. Can you speak to the sergeant on the main desk to assign a guard to our door, please? No non-medical personnel are to be admitted."

I left his office with a skip in my step. At last, something interesting was happening in this dark dungeon! Professor Simpson confirmed that he would attend at nine the following morning, so Doctor Bow had us all scrubbing, cleaning, and filing away our current crop of corpses. A clerk was dispatched to the ruined apartment block where the deceased woman been recovered from to find some clues to her identity.

I walked a different route back to the house I shared with some other single, male medical staff, passing a red phone box. Early evening had settled in, and the sun was turning a shade of orange over the rooftops of West London. I punched a couple of pennies into the slot and dialled Alice's number. One of her housemates answered.

"She's not in, I'm afraid. In fact, she didn't return to her duties at the hospital after her lunch break."

My heart skipped and I found myself holding my breath. After a moment, I replied, "I was with her at lunch. We parted at the end of Kensington High Street, and I saw her walk up Hornton Street towards the town hall. She was definitely heading back to work."

"Well, she didn't arrive. I work alongside her, and we were rushed off our feet all afternoon. But it's unlike her to disappear without warning."

I chewed my lip and wondered what to say next. "If she shows up, can you please ask her to call me? I'll be worried about her until I know that she's safe."

"Why wouldn't she be safe? Is there anything I should know?"

"Oh no, I just meant... you know, with all the bomb craters around..."

"Yes, of course. You're a good friend for worrying about her. But I wouldn't want to mess with Alice. She can stick up for herself. I'm sure she'll turn up. I'll pass the message on..."

The pips went, signalling that my money was running out. "Alright, thank you, Sandra." Then the line went dead. A woman was waiting so I held the door open for her. Across the road, the man in the navy greatcoat was looking at me, taking the last drag on a cigarette. "Hey! I want to talk to you!" I yelled as I ran into the road.

A car's screeching brakes brought me to a standstill. "Oi, watch where you're going!" the driver yelled as the tiny Austin picked up speed again, leaving me shocked on the edge of the concrete road slab. By the time I'd composed myself, the man was gone. I looked both ways and ran across the road, then down a side road that led towards some warehouses by the river.

As I turned the corner, there was a pile of rubble and the shattered foundations of what was once a warehouse. Beyond that, the brown flow of the Thames, impervious to the human carnage that littered its banks. In the centre of the rubble was the remains of the fuselage of a German Heinkel bomber, with the glass nose twisted and broken. A boy sat in the cockpit, twisting the bull's horns of the steering yoke in an imagined dodge from a *Hurricane* or *Spitfire*.

"Did you see a tall man in a greatcoat run by just now?"

"I ain't seen nuffin', Mister," came the reply.

I skirted around the warehouse complex but saw no one except a friendly watchman who gave another version of the boy's reply. Was I imagining it? I only saw him for a fleeting moment, and then he was gone. Could he have followed Alice instead of me? My head was a swirl of doom-laden thoughts as I traipsed home.

Our housekeeper and cook, Mrs Higgins, served dinner at precisely seven o'clock each evening, and I joined the assembled hungry young men to devour a rich rabbit stew with carrots, turnips, and potatoes, and a slice of bread to wipe the plate clean.

"I managed to get two fresh bucks from the butchers this morning," she had proudly announced. We'd handed over our ration cards to her and she saw to all our dietary needs, including biscuits and a sandwich for lunch on request. The phone didn't ring that evening, and I went to bed in a sombre mood, resolving to call Alice's workstation during the mid-morning break.

That night I dreamt of the Blackout Ripper, creeping up on an unsuspecting woman and pouncing, like a cat on a mouse. I awoke to the distant sound of anti-aircraft fire, and searchlights criss-crossing the sky through the thin curtains. It was over Kent, miles away.

My unsettled mind then turned to the great question of the day: what could our leaders have done differently to have avoided becoming the focus of the murderous rage of Adolf Hitler? Every night for three months up to the end of 1940, the Luftwaffe had returned, like the fallen angels of Hell, to bomb us out of existence. They hadn't succeeded, despite the terrible destruction and loss of life, but their raids continued on a sporadic basis, keeping us in a constant state of dread. Finding some comfort in the selfish thought that tonight some other poor souls were cowering in shelters, I took a sip of water and returned to my bed.

*****

Professor Simpson had the bearing of an important man. His bald head with stripes of grey above each ear nodded respectfully as he digested the briefing from a visibly perspiring Doctor Bow. The identity of the woman had been established as Mrs Jennifer Molyneux, the widow of Royal Navy Chief Petty Officer, Ralph Molyneux. She had lived alone in their apartment off Kensington High Street, following news of his being missing, presumed dead.

Doctor Bow looked accusingly at me and said, "Our junior Doctor Robinson, here, had given the victim a perfunctory roadside examination after she was brought from the bombed ruins of her apartment building. He thought he noticed signs of a possible assault and had the ambulance crew bring her here for further examination. On examining her myself, I felt there was enough due cause to classify the unfortunate woman as a suspicious death and call for your esteemed expertise." He wrung his hands, as if cleansing himself of any responsibility in the matter.

Professor Simpson, almost the age-mate of Doctor Bow, but taller, leaner, and in a fitter condition, raised his eyes from the clean red floor tiles and met my stare. "You did the right thing, Doctor Robinson. It's always better to err on the side of caution in these matters and seek additional advice. You may assist me in the post-mortem."

I shot a nervous grin in the direction of Doctor Bow, who appeared less than pleased. As the senior man, he would have expected to have been invited to assist the coroner. With a barely perceptible bow, he withdrew.

"You know, forensic science is in its infancy, Robinson. A fascinating subject, and one that elevates the rank of the medical professional to that of sleuth. We'll examine the victim to ascertain the likely cause of death, and if we suspect foul play, we'll call the police. Now, wash your hands and remove her garments."

Professor Simpson dictated his findings to a clerk who scribbled furiously on a pad.

"The deceased's cranium has sustained a heavy blow to the rear, causing blood to have matted in the hair around the wound. The congealed blood appears to be more than twenty-four hours old, pre-dating yesterday's air raid. I would estimate it was incurred during the previous night or the day before. The wound itself has pierced the cranium and appears to have been made with a solid object with a pointed end. It could have been sustained by falling backwards onto a solid object, such as the corner of a fireguard, or by a blow to the head from an instrument such as a masonry hammer. There are dark rings around her eyes and on raising her eye lids, I note that her sclerae are bloodshot, due to excessive stress, irritation, conjunctivitis, or possibly as a consequence of strangulation."

He turned to me and whispered, "That will be for the police to determine on further investigation. But there is a case here to be investigated." He winked.

Professor Simpson took a sip of tea and continued, "The victim's neck bears bruising consistent with finger impressions from a right hand, thus." He hovered his hand over the woman's neck and turned to me with a grin. "And now we come to the arms and wrists. No fractures but mild bruising on the upper arms. The hands, however, have bruising on the knuckles and the fingernails are broken or chipped, with blood encrusted under them. Perhaps the blood of her assailant."

Again, he turned and whispered to me, "She put up a fight alright. Poor thing."

He continued with an examination of the whole body, right down to her toes, but found nothing out of the ordinary. "So, in conclusion, the victim was discovered curled up on the floor of her lounge after an air raid had blown out the front wall of the building. There are no shrapnel wounds, so cause of death isn't as a result of a bomb blast. However, there are signs of a possible assault. I'm returning a verdict of suspicious death and will notify the police."

After scrubbing his hands and his implements, he packed up his bag and was off, leaving us to attend to the row of bodies on trollies in the corridor that were waiting for our attention.

I was pleased to have had the opportunity to assist the great Professor Simpson in a post-mortem examination and felt justified in my actions that had brought this case under the spotlight. I resolved to study up on forensic examinations and case studies of doctors working on police investigations. Perhaps this could open up a new career path for me. At eleven o'clock, I excused myself for a break and went to the pay phone near the main entrance. I called Alice's workplace, and the extension rang for a minute before someone picked up.

"I'm sorry to disturb you. This is Doctor Robinson from Charing Cross Hospital. May I have a word with Doctor Alice Wilson please?" I held my breath.

A female colleague replied, "I'm afraid Doctor Wilson didn't report for work this morning. Can anyone else help you?"

It was the reply that I was dreading to hear, and it felt like a knife had pierced my heart. "Erm, no. Can I speak to one of the women that she shares a house with? Sandra is one…"

"We're all frightfully busy at the moment, Doctor Robinson. Can you call again later?"

I came off the phone even more worried than before; an awful stomach cramp caused me to bend forward.

"Are you alright, Martin?" a passing doctor asked. "You look awfully pale. Do you have a stomach ache?"

"I've… just received some bad news."

"I could ask old Bow Tie to let you go early," he offered.

I grimaced and he hurried off. Old Bow Tie wouldn't look favourably on me after the slight he'd received at the hands of haughty coroner. But I should at least try, whilst I still looked pale and felt queasy.

I knocked on his door and he muttered, "Come in. Ah, it's you, Robinson. A budding coroner in the making." There was sarcasm in his smile.

"I've come over all queer, sir. Stomach cramps and feverish."

"Well, stay away from me, young man. I suggest you go up to the second floor and see the day nurse. If she gives you medication and recommends that you rest, then sleep it off on her couch."

I collected my coat, hat, and gas mask and left the basement, climbing the circular stairs up two floors. The nurse took my temperature and said I was slightly warm, but not feverish. She gave me a pill to settle my stomach cramp and an aspirin for pain relief, washed down with a tumbler of water. As predicted, she told me to take off my shoes and lie on the bed in a side room for half an hour, and then return to her for review. I duly complied, but as soon as she'd left and closed the connecting door, I put my shoes on and left.

Retracing my steps from yesterday, I came to the junction where Alice and I had parted. Whirlwinds of dust blew merrily in the doorways and vacant plots on Kensington High Street, on an otherwise warm and bright spring day. I marched up Hornton Street towards the town hall, pausing at a bomb site where a Georgian period townhouse once stood, judging by the adjacent houses, no doubt occupied by relieved neighbours. Children played in the ruins, running around a rubble pile with wooden aeroplanes, chasing each other in mock dog fights.

"Excuse me, did any of you see a young woman pass this way around this time yesterday?"

They stopped and stared in sullen silence, annoyed at the interruption.

"Were any of you here yesterday?" I persisted.

A boy with a stick glared defiantly at me. "I've been here every day since Christmas, Mister."

"Yeah, he keeps out of his ma's way, so she don't send 'im back to the farm. He's a 'vacuee," his pal added.

"He says they beat him in Kent." This was almost whispered by a bespectacled girl.

'I'm sorry to hear that, but I'm only interested in yesterday. This is very important. Think carefully. Did you see a woman go past here, a very pretty woman with thick, golden curls?"

They shook their heads and ran off. I re-focussed my troubled mind on the obstacles on my route as I passed the town hall and its sandbag shelter. Cracked and split pavement slabs were a constant hazard, making any walk an obstacle course. I entered Fulham Hospital and my doctor's pass satisfied the glum soldier on the reception desk. I noted the folded right sleeve where there was once an arm and wondered if he'd been right-handed and had to learn to write again with his left. Alice's department was on the first floor, and the nurse on the desk remembered me.

"Ah, Doctor Robinson. If you've come looking for Alice, she's not here."

"Any idea where she might be?"

"None. She didn't go home last night and none of her housemates have seen her or know where she might be. Odd. She's not one for unannounced absences. Although, now I think of it, an American officer was pestering her for a date. I do hope she's alright."

"You and me both. How long before she can be reported missing?"

"Our admin staff start investigating after two days' absence without leave, and contact the other hospitals in the area. The police are usually only involved on the third day. We've lost a few to air raids."

"I can imagine. Well, I can confirm she survived yesterday's bombing, as we met for lunch after."

"I'll pass a note to that effect onto the admin crew. Can I get you a tea?"

"No, thanks. I'll be off. Can you ask your admin people to call her mother's house in Reigate? I think I'll visit her lodgings this evening. Thanks anyway."

With that, I withdrew and roamed the streets for an hour before going home. Chatted up by an American officer, eh? Perhaps I'd pass by some of the clubs frequented by the army officers in the evening. Levels of worry and anxiety just seemed to pile up, the daily gripes aggravated and amplified by the grave national emergency that was playing out.

I wandered along Kensington High Street and saw that the square had been partially tidied up. The cherry blossom tree had been chopped down. This time, George Washington was in the clear, but its untimely death was a bad omen. I felt so miserable and doom-laden that I entered St Mary's Church and lit a candle. I knelt at the rail to the Lady Chapel and clenched my hands in silent prayer that dear, sweet Alice would be found unharmed. An involuntary sob was accompanied by a lone tear that ran down my dry cheek. I'd only lost an uncle to the war so far, but now the thought of losing someone close struck me with anxiety and a deep sadness.

On my slow walk home, I reflected on the sense of duty that kept us all from falling apart, reinforced by government messaging. The company of my housemates partly lifted my spirits as tales of the day were exchanged. No meat in tonight's stew, but the dumplings were a comfort. Fortified, I went out and visited all the clubs in Kensington, armed with a picture of Alice, but shakes of heads was all I got.

Alice still hadn't come home, and Sandra resolved to push admin to investigate in the morning and report her disappearance to the police if there was no news. Two mysteries in one day. Sleep came slowly, but in the end, my body succumbed, and I awoke refreshed, my loins girded for the unflinching fight.

*****

On the third night after Alice's disappearance, the Luftwaffe returned. The cat's wail of the siren cut short our evening meal and the eight of us scurried out through the kitchen door to the back yard. The Anderson shelter, built of brick with a corrugated tin roof had two rows of wooden benches which we sat on, facing each other, making bad jokes to lighten the moment. It was positioned to avoid the possibility of being crushed under a collapsing wall and designed to protect those inside from flying shrapnel. But we all feared the possibility of a direct hit. Trains remained in the stations as the railway line behind was calmed in the cowering silence.

The next day, I traipsed up to Hammersmith Police Station and asked the desk sergeant if there was any news on the disappearance of Doctor Alice Wilson, four days missing now. He grunted and looked in the daybook.

"Her disappearance was only reported yesterday, along with twelve others. We've only got one detective here, assisted by a couple of constables." His pale blue eyes spoke of weary resignation.

"I could have been the last person to have seen her."

"I'll see if there's anyone who can take your statement, sir. Please sit over there." He nodded in the direction of a wooden bench. After thirty minutes of thumb twitching, I returned to the desk and told the sergeant I'd have to report back for work. He gave me a lined pad and a pencil, and asked me to write a short statement, sign, and date it, giving my contact details. Duly completed, I ran back to the mortuary.

"There's a couple waiting to see you," old Bow Tie growled through his open door as I tried to slip past. "You know our policy on personal visitors during working hours, Doctor Robinson. Take a message, if there is one, and get rid of them. We've received eight bodies since last night's air raid."

I turned and ran up to the ground-floor reception area with a feeling of dread. Unexpected visitors during the day often spelt bad news. And there she was. I felt a flutter in my chest as my barely comprehending eyes fixed themselves on Alice. Dishevelled, forlorn, and sporting a bandage around her head, but Alice, nonetheless.

"Alice!" I shouted, rushing across the worn marble floor. She stood and fell into my embrace, the welcome aroma of her unwashed curls inhaled in a moment of validation mixed with pure joy. "I've been so worried…"

"Oh Martin, I'm so happy and relieved to see you again. Since our lunch… well, I don't really know where to begin." She turned her head to her companion, who stood, fingering a worn, brimmed hat.

"You!" I blurted out. It was the mystery man in the Royal Navy greatcoat.

The desk sergeant approached to add to my confusion. "Now then, Doctor Robinson, sir. No shouting. This is a hospital."

I looked from the sergeant to the mystery man, my overworked brain struggling to process what was happening. Having convinced myself that he was a figment of my imagination or a ghost, he was now standing in front of me, and in the company of my Alice, who I'd feared was dead.

"Come into the waiting room," Alice said, noting my confusion. "I'll explain." She took my arm and led me into a side room, followed by the mystery man, and closed the door. "This is Anthony Marshall, an able seaman. He was indeed following us after our lunch - he can explain why. But the important thing is, I lost my footing on the way back to work when a pavement slab gave way and I fell down a coal scuttle into a cellar. It was in a side street in a row of bombed out, abandoned houses. I was knocked out for a while but came to in Anthony's arms as he carried me to a hospital for treatment."

I gasped at her account. "You... fell into a cellar?"

"She smiled and squeezed my arm. "Yes. Next to a dead rat. I passed out again and woke up in a hospital bed." She paused to touch the bandage on the left side of her head. "But not my hospital. He carried me to Great Ormond Street. No one there knew me, and my ID card must have slipped out of my pocket. I was concussed and drifted in and out of sleep. I was too drowsy to worry that nobody there knew who I was. But on the second day, I started to have flashbacks of working in a hospital and thought I might be a nurse. Then yesterday, whilst I was sat out in the courtyard, Anthony returned to check up on me. He explained what had happened and told me he'd seen me with a man he was following who he'd discovered was... you. Doctor Martin Robinson."

I gasped and turned my gaze to the man in the greatcoat. "But why were you following me?"

He cleared his throat, as if to give a speech. "My apologies if I scared you, Doc. I was in a confused state, walking aimlessly. Then I decided to follow some Royal Navy uniforms, who entered the apartment block on Kensington High Street. I was struck by a vague feeling that I might've been there before. Perhaps I lived there or knew someone who did. You see, my ship was sunk at Dunkirk, and I washed up on the beach. I was evacuated back to Blighty and came to in a hospital bed with only a patchy memory of what had happened. My earlier life, I couldn't recall." His dark eyes searched the walls for meaning. "They sent me to convalesce in a home in Hampshire, but when bits of memories started to return, like flashbacks, I was keen to come to London to try and jolt my memory. Then after the air raid, I saw you, looking at the bombed flats. You looked at a body brought out of the ruins, as if you were looking for someone. For some reason, I thought you might recognise me or be able to help me."

"But why did you follow Alice rather than me, when we parted after lunch?" I asked, incredulous.

"Well… I followed you first to this hospital, then turned around and walked the route that Doctor Wilson had taken. Don't ask me why, I was still in a bit of a state. I'm not even sure myself. I just wanted to meet someone who knew me or could help me to remember."

"And it's just as well he did, or I may have been in that cellar all night," Alice added.

I exhaled deeply and held Alice by her shoulders. "Well, I can't say how relieved and happy I am to have you back, Alice." Her arms went around me in a mutually comforting hug.

After a brief silence, I looked up at the man again.

"I still have flashbacks of the explosion on my ship, but I can remember very little before that," he said, scratching his unruly mop of hair.

"And my memories are still a little fuzzy from before my accident, but I do remember our lunch, Martin." Her lower lip trembled, and her eyes filled with tears.

Before I could formulate a response, the man spoke again. "I think I might have gone AWOL, and wondered if I could ask you both, being doctors and all, to hand me in to the nearest army post? You can tell 'em you found me wanderin' dazed and confused."

"Well, I think it's the least we can do for you, Anthony," I shook his hand in acknowledgement that he was now friend and not foe. "You know, I wondered if you were real or a just figment of my imagination. This war is really messing with all of our heads."

"But at least one of your two mysteries is solved," Alice smiled, hooking her arm into mine.

Old Bow Tie gave me the rest of the afternoon off, on hearing a brief, garbled account of what had happened to Alice, and I walked with them to the army barracks at Hammersmith.

I approached the guard on duty and identified myself as a doctor, then introduced my "patient", Able Seaman Anthony Marshall, an amnesiac found wandering the streets. That should've been enough for him to escape a charge.

"Right. I'll be off then. Nice to have met you, Doctor Robinson, and to have been of assistance, Doctor Wilson," Anthony said, shaking our hands. Alice gave him a hug. He wandered into the barracks between two guards, another psychologically degraded warrior, his life-threatening mission not yet complete.

"Good luck!" I shouted after him.

"I can't imagine what he's been through, poor chap," Alice said, holding my arm tightly. "The nightmare of Dunkirk, then the terror of losing his memory."

I guided her past the stump of the cherry blossom tree, pausing briefly to pick up a dusty blossom, on our way to The Prince of Wales. Once settled in a corner booth with our drinks, we fell into familiar conversation.

"Does this place ring any bells? Or this blossom?"

She nodded, turning the delicate flower in her hand. "I remember you were in a hurry to solve a potential murder, Martin. What have you found out?"

"What I've found out is that sleuthing is a slow and frustrating business, and I'm not cut out for it. However, the coroner agreed with my theory that she had most likely been murdered. Your disappearance scared the wits out of me, and the poor woman's violent death will probably get scant attention, because there's not enough policemen. Faced with the urgent mystery of my missing girlfriend, I hardly knew where to start. You'd disappeared into thin air. I roamed the streets, one of the ranks of the desperate who've lost someone."

"So, I'm your girlfriend, am I?" Her eyes twinkled with mischief.

I surreptitiously patted the familiar lump of the jeweller's pouch in my jacket pocket.

"You know what I mean." I took a fierce interest in the depth of my pint glass.

She leaned towards me, like Mata Hari at a rendezvous. "As far as I know, you've been the only one retracing my footsteps, Martin."

"Is that good?"

Without a hint of her usual friendly mockery, she said, "It's marvellous."

Brian's Beat

Part One – When We Were Young

March 1966. England was in the grip of football fever as the country prepared to host the World Cup. In London, teenage boys in ironed, white shirts, inch-wide ties, and pleated trousers lounged around, leaning against the wall outside The Electric Ballroom in Camden Town on a balmy spring evening, eyeing up the girls in their colourful dresses - the hemlines having recently moved up to expose knees and thighs.

The two groups exchanged banter in a timeless mating ritual; coquettish glances and shy giggles elicited macho poses from strutting cocks who'd combed up their Brylcreemed hair and were dragging on their tabs, nonchalantly flicking the stubs in the general direction of the gutter.

Brian Smith knew who he was after. A pretty, little blonde girl called Helen who he knew from school. She was one year his junior, but was no longer a geeky schoolgirl - she had blossomed into an attractive young woman, and he was determined to ask her to dance. That was the protocol. Bundle inside, pay your sixpence at the box office, get a paper cup of fruit punch, and line the walls with your mates, waiting for the hall to fill and the jazz band to strike up a familiar tune. Brian combed back his brown quiff and pushed off the wall, with a "Good luck, mate" from a friend to bolster his nerve.

The crowds seemed to part in front of him as he crossed the hall. Her friends whispered and giggled as she looked up - it was as if she'd been waiting for him. He held her wide, blue-eyed gaze and asked, "Would you like to dance?"

"I can't jive," she said. Her friends laughed as if it was the funniest joke ever, buying Brian a few seconds to formulate his next move.

"Then let's get some punch and wait for the next one," he said, taking her firmly by the arm and leading her away from her friends. "Always try to separate them from their mates," was the advice that came to mind, given by one of the older boys.

"Are you always so forceful?" she asked, sipping her drink, and glancing over at her jealous friends.

"I'm not a kid anymore... I'm joining the police next week," he said. This was designed to impress her, and it worked; it signalled responsibility and a steady job.

"I like this one," she said, as the band played a popular hit. This time, it was Helen doing the leading, as the infatuated couple found a space and held each other in a classic dance pose.

"It all seemed so easy," Brian told his mates the next day. "As if it was meant to be. We're going out now, so no comments or whistles."

Brian had transitioned seamlessly from hanging out with mischief in mind to enrolling at police training college and being in a steady relationship. He even put his name down for a council flat. In those heady days of youth, everything seemed possible, and his world was full of firsts. First girlfriend; first job; first pay cheque; first passport; first holiday; and soon after, marriage and first home of their own.

Brian would twirl his police whistle in the pub for laughs but cautioned his mates on their behaviour. He had the cocky confidence of his hero, football captain Bobby Moore - and each morning his feet slipped effortlessly into his size nine boots, as if this was always meant to be.

Although based at Camden, Brian was seconded to a team of bobbies who had the important task of policing the queues of people at Westminster Hall in Central London where the Jules Rimet Trophy was on display, looking glorious, but rather out of place amongst a stamp collection. That was the name of the World Cup Trophy, a beautifully carved trophy that could be held in one hand, made of sterling silver and plated with 24-carat gold.

Brian gawped at the iconic trophy, displayed on a plinth in a glass case, hoping that it would be his hero, Bobby Moore, who would lift it up after winning the World Cup final at Wembley Stadium in July. That was just a dream in March 1966, but with a home advantage, surely England had a good chance. Brian shifted his position to negate the glare from the spotlight reflections until he could see the detail of the intricately carved lines on the goddess holding up a globe. In the briefing, they'd been told that its value, for insurance purposes, was a million pounds.

The exhibition opened on Saturday, 19 March, and Brian spent the day outside, watching curious members of the public file respectfully through the grand, high doorway of the fifty-year-old building that shared its use between being an exhibition hall and a Methodist church. Inside the exhibition hall, the four security guards seemed overwhelmed by the volume of people at this hastily arranged exhibition of the World Cup Trophy. It had been a last-minute idea from someone at the Football Association, so the Metropolitan Police were quickly mobilised for crowd control.

Brian laughed and joked with the football fans, recognising some of his team-mates and fellow West Ham supporters who slowly shuffled into the cool interior for a once-in-a-lifetime chance to see the famous trophy for free.

"You playin' termorra? one of the lads from Camden Town FC asked.

"Na, mate, I'm on duty 'ere," Brian replied with a grin. "Shame I'll miss it, but the overtime will come in handy."

The following morning, Brian was separating two arguing men by the main entrance, when a cry went up from inside the hall. A few seconds later, one of the security guards ran out and shouted at him, "The World Cup Trophy's been stolen!"

Brian stared in disbelief at the white-haired, old man and asked, "Are you sure?" He'd been wondering the day before why two of the four guards were past retirement age and if they were up to guarding such a valuable exhibit.

"Of course I'm sure! Two fellas smashed the glass and made off wiv' it through the fire exit!" His rheumy eyes were wide, and his arm was pointing inside.

Brian pulled out his whistle and blew a series of loud blasts. The three other policemen on his shift came running up the stone steps to him as the alarmed crowd stood back and gawped. There were no police inside, only the four guards.

Their shift leader was Sergeant Morrison, and he took charge. "Right, lads, let's get inside and inspect the crime scene and see what can be done."

Brian's eyes gradually adjusted to the darker interior as the metal tacks on the soles of his boots rang a tune on the ceramic tile floor as he followed his sergeant along a corridor and into the large exhibition hall. They barged through the milling crowd to the display plinth and saw the shattered glass on the floor and the empty cabinet. Behind, the doors to a fire exit were open. Three sorry-looking guards stood to one side.

"Smith and Collins, get after them!" Sergeant Morrison commanded.

Brian and his fellow new recruit ran to the emergency exit, hearing the loud voice of their sergeant behind them questioning the guards. Brian grinned to his mate as they heard one of the guards squeak, "…but we were on our tea break when it happened!"

Outside in the weak, spring sunlight, they looked both ways along the street, then decided to split up and run in separate directions. Brian asked passersby on his way if they'd seen men running away from the exhibition hall. None of them had, some merely shook their heads. After half an hour, Brian returned to the hall. Sergeant Morrison was still berating the cowering guards.

"So, let's get this straight," the grizzled ex-soldier thundered, "you were all absent from the room on tea break at the same time! I can hardly believe it. So, the thieves must've had a man inside the hall waiting for his chance to push open the emergency exit doors, and you just gave it to him. The others were waiting outside. So simple a plan my gran could've made it up. Smith, did you see anyone running or get any reports of the men?"

"No, sarge," Brian panted, trying to get his wind back.

Just then, PC Collins returned, blurting out his news. "Sarge! I spoke to a couple who saw a Hillman Minx, beige colour, pulling away in a hurry after two men jumped in the back."

"Good lad. Any numbers or letters of the registration?"

Collins shook his head.

"Alright, now get statements from this useless lot and any witnesses in the room. I'll call in the report to the chief inspector. This'll give him indigestion."

Over the next few days, Brian raced around London with teams of coppers in a frantic search of the hideouts of known criminals. "Organised crime gangs, I'm sure of it," the chief inspector had swiftly concluded, with no apparent leads or evidence. "Round up our snitches; someone's gotta know something," he'd barked in the meeting the following morning.

Brian learned sometime later that the Football Association, panicking at the loss of the trophy three months before the tournament, had commissioned a replica to be made. In the end, it wasn't needed, as, despite a false ransom claim that led to the arrest of a conman, by pure luck, the trophy was found abandoned by the roadside by a man walking his dog. It was the dog, a collie called Pickles, that had drawn his owner to a package wrapped up with string, and to his surprise, the World Cup Trophy was in it. Being an honest citizen, he handed it in at his nearest police station.

Brian took up the story with his mates in the pub a few weeks after. The unimpressed desk sergeant had said, 'Doesn't look very World Cuppy to me, son'." Brian's mates fell about laughing and it earned him a refill of his pint.

"As for Pickles the collie," Brian continued after a mouthful of beer, "he's going to become a TV star, when he appears on *Blue Peter* and he's been nominated for Dog of the Year… and I've shaken his paw."

The World Cup was played without incident, and Pickles was the hero who had saved England's hosting of the prestigious event from ignominy and ridicule. Brian's hero, Bobby Moore, was to lift the famous trophy on 30 July at Wembley Stadium after defeating Germany, England's traditional rivals, in the final. All was rosy in PC Brian's garden and the warm glow of victory carried him through an otherwise uneventful first year.

Part Two – Let It Be

A bright, chilly January morning in 1969 saw Brian on the West End beat. Rounding the corner into Savile Row, he found a small crowd gathering outside Apple Records, the headquarters of the world-famous pop group, The Beatles. As the first bobby on the scene, he asked a young man what was going on.

"We've heard a rumour that The Beatles are going to play on the rooftop," the excited youth said.

PC Brian Smith radioed it in and was told to enter the building and wait for further instructions. He squeezed past busy roadies carrying equipment up three steps and into the narrow front door of what was a large, grey stone converted townhouse, glancing at a row of framed gold records on the walls before his eyes settled on the receptionist. Her pretty face, heavily made-up with Mary Quant mascara on her long lashes, framed by a lacquered brown bob, wore a pensive look. She hesitated before confirming that the band would be giving a brief performance of their new songs on the rooftop.

"Can I see the manager please?" Brian asked, showing initiative.

"Would that be the general manager for Apple Records or the manager of The Beatles?" she asked, holding a white phone to her neck.

"Erm, both, if I may … Emily," he said stiffly, leaning forward to read her name on a green apple badge.

She punched some numbers on her switchboard and spoke in a quiet voice. "A police officer would like to see you."

Brian gazed over her head at the pictures of his music heroes, the Fab Four. The smell of weed drifted into the room from what looked like the post room behind reception. Emily, seeing him sniff the air, hurriedly pushed the door shut.

"Mr Taylor, the general manager, will see you in his office. You'll have to walk up the stairs, I'm afraid, as there's no lift. All the way to the fourth floor, then left at the top of the stairs."

Brian thanked her and followed a film crew carrying camera equipment and tripods up the narrow staircase. His radio crackled into life, and he stepped into the first-floor corridor to improve the reception. His Sergeant told him there was no record of an application to hold a public performance on the rooftop but was unsure if they'd be breaking any laws by doing so in their own building, unless it was so loud that it caused a disturbance.

"Find out what you can and report back," he said tersely. "I'm sending more bobbies for crowd control outside the building."

Brian looked about him and saw the name "John" on an office door. He pushed the door open and found himself looking straight at a long-haired, bespectacled John Lennon leaning back in a swivel chair, feet on a cluttered desk, smoking a joint.

"Oh, hell, is this a raid?" he asked, looking momentarily startled as he saw Brian's uniform.

"Erm, no, Mr Lennon. I'm just here to find out about this concert on the roof. Would you mind telling me what it's all about?"

John pointed to a chair and sat up, squeezing the lit end of his joint and throwing it in a bin.

"Sorry about that, officer...?"

"PC Brian Smith," he said, easing himself into a leather armchair, cradling his helmet in his arms. "Oh, don't worry about that, I'm a big fan, you know."

"Glad to hear it," John said, leaning over the desk to shake his hand. "We've just decided to play some of our latest tunes for our next album on the roof and make a promo film, if you know what I mean?"

"Erm, yes, but if you make too much noise, you'll disturb the other businesses in the area, and we're bound to get complaints. My boss tells me that you haven't notified the police, and a crowd is already gathering in the street, so maybe…"

John got to his feet and put his arm around Brian's shoulders. "Look, PC Brian, it's just a few songs and it won't take long. Why don't you come up onto the roof and watch? We won't make that much noise, honest. You see, the wind will carry our music away, up into the ether." He waved a hand theatrically over his head as he guided Brian up the stairs, collecting the other Beatles as he went.

"You see, Brian, each of us has our own floor, 'cause we can't stand the sight of each other after ten years together, ain't that right, Ringo?"

The mop-topped drummer grinned sheepishly as John gathered each group member as they made their way to the roof. Once up there, Brian saw the instruments and speakers set up on a wooden platform, and the camera crew buzzing around their equipment.

"We're nearly ready, John," said a smartly dressed man who looked like he was in charge. He smiled at Brian and held out his hand. "Hi, I'm George Martin. Why don't you come over here with me? We'll be starting in a few minutes."

Brian's radio crackled and he heard his sergeant saying, "They've barricaded the door, and we can't get in, what's happening, Smith?"

"I can't hear you, sir, I'll try and move to get a better reception." He grinned at George and clipped his radio onto his belt, turning the sound dial down.

After a brief soundcheck, The Beatles started playing. Brian looked down to the street below and saw the crowd had built up considerably, as workers on their lunch break began to converge around the building. Brian knew it would only be a matter of time before his colleagues managed to gain entry. In fact, he'd listened to five songs with great enthusiasm before the first of the officers barged their way onto the roof. Turning to George, Brian asked, "How much time do you need?"

George smiled and replied, "We're almost through. Thanks for your support. About ten minutes should do it."

Brian pushed his way over to a burly sergeant and said, "I've told them to wind it up, sarge. They're making a short promotional film for their new album. Just a few more minutes." The sergeant glared at him but said nothing. The Beatles were playing their third take of "Get Back" and Paul, seeing that their time was up, cheekily changed the lyrics - "You've been playing on the roof again, and you know your momma doesn't like it, she's gonna have you arrested."

At the end of the song, John approached the microphone and droned sardonically in his nasal manner: "I'd like to say thank you on behalf of myself and the group, and I hope we've passed the audition."

Brian turned to George Martin, who thanked him and shook his hand.

"What will the album be called?" Brian asked.

"Not sure yet, it'll either be *Get Back* or *Let it Be*," Martin replied.

Brian filed downstairs behind the line of policemen. He would stick to his story that he'd negotiated a swift end to the impromptu gig. It was a memory that he would carry with him, much more than another pub story, it was a sense that he'd been part of something special that somehow crowned the swinging sixties, and that he was one of the very few privileged people to witness it. After all, The Beatles had practically written the soundtrack to the Sixties. It was to be The Beatles' last ever performance, which made it more of a poignant landmark in his London life. It left him with a sense of belonging; a sense of pride; a sense of time and place and his own location on the historical conveyor belt of this great city.

Part Three – The Stakeout

"It was a Sunday morning I'll never forget," Brian said. "A warm September day in 1971. Not unlike today, in fact. I was a fresh-faced detective constable at the time, much like yourself." He turned to view the profile of his young protégé, sitting next to him in the unmarked police car. The stakeout was already dragging on.

DC Philip Clark's bored gaze was fixed on an upstairs bedroom window and a hand making a small gap in the curtains to peer through. "But you never got them," he said.

Detective Sergeant Brian Smith exhaled and tapped his finger on the dashboard. "No, we never got them. Eight million quid's worth lifted from the safety deposit boxes of the guilty rich. Almost a victimless crime. We always suspected they had someone on the inside. A bent copper."

Clark turned to face him. "Any idea who it was?"

Brian popped a crisp into his mouth and stared ahead. "Some movement at the front door," he said. Clark lifted his camera and started snapping as a man and woman emerged, blinking in the sunlight. "Radio it in, Clark," he said, starting the engine, adding, "The cheeky bastards left a message for us painted on the bank vault wall – 'Let's see how Sherlock Holmes solves this'."

They slowly followed the walking couple at a discreet distance. "What's the relevance of Sherlock Holmes?" Clark asked innocently.

"You really don't know, do you?" Brian replied. "The bank was on Baker Street, that's why."

Clark laughed. "That's funny, Sherlock Holmes!"

"Yeah, he would have been handy. We had DI Alex Jones who seemed to do everything in his power to mess it up. We were made to look like the Keystone Cops."

The couple flagged down a taxi and jumped in. Brian followed. "Call for another car to join us - let's mix it up a bit."

They followed the taxi all the way over Tower Bridge and the two pursuing cars pulled in behind it outside a tall, dilapidated warehouse building off Borough High Street. The couple got out and entered the building. "Speak of the devil," Brian said, as Chief Inspector Jones emerged from the car behind and approached them.

"Morning, sir," Brian said through his open window.

"Morning, Smith. Who's your young apprentice?"

"This is DC Clark, sir. His first stakeout."

The sun shone off Jones's bald pate as he leaned in. "Right, I want you, Clark, round the back and you, Smith, come with me in the front. Let's move."

"Be careful," Brian cautioned his eager partner. "They're part of a drugs gang, so they might have shooters. Hang back and observe, alright?" Clark nodded and they moved off.

"Shouldn't we wait for backup, sir?" Brian whispered as it became apparent there were a dozen men attending this meeting, and they were heavily outnumbered.

"You stay there, Smith. The drug squad's on its way. I'm going to get a better look." Jones was now in his sixties and had been behind a desk for the last ten years. Brian was puzzled by the presence of a senior officer as he watched his suited superior move away towards the back of the warehouse in a crouched shuffle.

"What's he up to?" Brian muttered as Jones disappeared behind a row of wooden crates.

Some sort of exchange was going on. Brian was worried now. There was no sign of backup arriving and Brian and his fellow officers were unarmed. He decided to look for the chief inspector. Imitating his crouched shuffle, he moved along a line of packing crates. He could hear voices and the occasional laugh about fifty feet away.

After five minutes, Brian reached the end of the line of crates, and was now to the side of the group, who were lined up in two rows of five, the rear row being armed gunmen holding automatic weapons. They were facing the couple from the taxi, who appeared to be negotiating a price for two suitcases positioned between the two parties. Movement to his right revealed Jones's location. Brian also made eye contact with Clark who was hiding in the gloom at the rear of the building. Brian waved his hand, indicating that Clark should join him.

Brian crept to Jones' side, and noted the senior man was bent over an open suitcase. Brian could see bundles of bank notes and knew exactly what it was.

"What's going on, sir?" Brian whispered to a flustered Jones.

"Nothing, Smith. I've just found this case and I'm checking the contents." He looked annoyed at being discovered. Brian knew it was a payoff. Most likely a pre-arranged pick-up for his services. His suspicions about DI Jones were confirmed in that instant. He was the one who had tipped off the bank robbers and was now collecting his reward. Clark approached but tripped, making a noise that alerted the gang.

"Oi! Who's there?" someone shouted, their voice echoing off the high, steel girders above their heads making some pigeons take flight.

Brian could see a side door close by and started to move towards it. "Let's go," he hissed, shuffling off. Looking back, he saw Clark helping Jones to his feet and follow behind. Brian forced open the door and urged the others to hurry as two armed men leapt over the packing cases and pointed their guns at them. A burst of automatic fire sent more birds flying into the air and Brian diving for cover. Jones took a bullet and fell with a cry, the case spilling open and bank notes attempted to take to the air, but, like incomplete birds, soon fluttered around the two kneeling men. Clark hesitated for a moment, then responded to Brian's urgent command to run. He made it to the door and Brian pulled him through.

"What about the chief inspector?" a wide-eyed Clark panted. They looked back to see Jones desperately shovelling the bank notes into the suitcase, as the two gunmen came to his side.

"They've got him. Best we can do is wait for armed response. Come on." Brian pulled a wide-eyed Clark by the sleeve and ran around the side of the building. More police cars had arrived on the scene and Brian waved his badge at an armed police officer. "DS Smith - there's an armed gang inside, about a dozen of them!" he shouted. "They've taken Chief Inspector Jones hostage."

Brian guided his young partner behind the police cordon and said, "Don't look so worried. There's been no more shots fired, and I think Jones was only wounded, so they're probably holding him. Nothing more we could have done. He shouldn't have led us in there without backup."

Brian reported to the senior officer in charge and told them about Jones and the case of neatly stacked bank notes, still with the bank's banding on them. They accepted plastic cups of tea and sat behind an armoured van. Brian turned to Clark and whispered, "I think 'Sherlock Jones' has finally been rumbled. Let's see him try and talk his way out of this one."

Part Four – The Waters of Time

"I don't get it," Del said, making no effort to conceal his boredom. "It's just a bath with dangling, coloured tubes." He was only two weeks into a work placement. It was 1981 and the government had rolled out a youth opportunity training scheme for school leavers to have their first taste of working life and reduce the ranks of the unemployed register that had passed the unwelcome mark of three million.

"Modern art, mate; now pay attention to the punters, not the items," Brian growled. The grizzled ex-cop had bellied out with a cushy job as a security guard at a prestigious London gallery following his early retirement after twenty-five years at the Met. They drifted away from *The Waters of Time*.

"You know, when I was your age," Brian said, his eyes scanning left to right, "my first job was guarding the World Cup Trophy."

"Oh yeah? How did that go?" the pimply youth replied.

"Not that well. Some villains nicked it. But we got it back. That's why we're here, son. To nip temptation in the bud. Now keep yer eyes peeled."

"My gran used to have one of those old iron bathtubs," Del airily commented as he scanned the steady flow of tourists and corralled schoolkids.

Brian scowled, not convinced that his young charge had listened to his anecdote. "Her old bathtub might be worth a few bob to one of these artists." He stopped and grabbed Del's arm, pointing. A woman in a broad-brimmed hat and sunglasses was looking about furtively as she reached into her bag. They closed the distance across the crowded gallery floor, but not in time to stop her stepping over the rope and spraying a political symbol in yellow paint across an old master.

"Oi! Come here!" Brian yelled, as he broke into a waddle. "Del, head her off!" he shouted, pointing to the exit.

She exploded into the modern art gallery, and seeing her way blocked by the young guard, she twisted, lost her balance, and tumbled into the iron bathtub. The two guards converged, and Del instinctively reached for his phone, snapping her flailing form as she battled with the tubing in her struggle to escape from *The Waters of Time*.

Brian looked over his young apprentice's shoulder at the photo he'd taken of the stricken woman. Big sunglasses on an angry face, enveloped by coloured tubing.

"Nice… now that's what I call a work of art."

Part Five – Nelson's End

Loud yells accompanied by hydraulic pumping forced Brian to close the lounge window, in spite of the stifling heat. The rhythm of life on the Camden council estate ebbed and flowed - it was a persistent tide of activity. The binmen gone, he opened the window again and breathed in the fetid, polluted air, slapping his fat, sweaty belly. The doorbell chimed and he moved slowly from the light into a dark corridor.

"Morning, Mr, er, Smith. I'm Pavel from housing association; I've come to service your boiler." The twenty-something blond-haired man looked up from his clipboard and smiled.

Brian had to back into the bedroom doorway to make enough space for the young Pole to squeeze past. "In there," he said, pointing in the only direction possible.

Brian wedged his generous belly in front of his tiny desk and continued with his coin audit, hoping for some peace so he could concentrate. In reality, he simply loved holding the old coins in his cotton-gloved hands and reading the inscriptions through an eyepiece. He had an inventory open in Excel on his laptop and would check each coin against its entry. After thirty minutes, Pavel came into the lounge.

"All done, Mr Smith. Everything's okay." He looked up at a framed wedding photo on the sideboard and added, "You look very happy there."

Brian spun around and saw the line of his gaze. "Oh yes. Nearly forty years since that was taken. My Helen, she passed away three years ago. Cancer took her, poor girl."

Pavel's face switched from cheery to horror. "I'm so sorry, sir. I didn't mean to …"

"It's alright. I always smile when I look at it. Happy days."

Pavel's eyes moved to the pictures on the wall. "These nice pictures of London with silver coins."

Brian stood and approached the wall, pointing to each of the four quadrants in turn: "These are limited edition, silver one hundred-pound coins, issued by the Royal Mint. Top left is Nelson's Column, then Big Ben, Buckingham Palace, and the Tower of London." Each coin was set against a pictorial background. Brian had lovingly framed his various coin sets and displayed them around the room. "Too nice to keep in a drawer," he muttered, by way of explanation.

"Very nice, Mr Smith. You have nice collection." Pavel smiled, relieved to have changed the subject to something lighter. "Maybe they will make coins for new buildings like Canary Wharf Tower," he added.

Brian snorted. "Perhaps they'll follow, but for now, it's just historic London. I'm not sure I would be so enthusiastic to pay homage to the glass towers of capitalism. To me, they're a reminder of a lost society - one that was based more on human values, community, and less on greed and graft." He looked up at the boiler-suited workman and laughed at his quizzical look.

"Don't worry, Pavel. I'm just being a silly, sentimental old bugger. Yes, the glass towers of capitalism is a good call for a coin or stamp series to mark the millennium."

He led the young man to the door and thanked him for the boiler service. "Glad to know I'm safe now!"

His policeman's instincts woke him with a jolt in the early hours. The rustle of the Venetian blinds had dragged him from his slumber. He swung his podgy legs over the side of the bed, wiggling his toes as he felt for his slippers, then turned on his bedside light. Four in the morning. "Must have left the damned window open," he muttered as he stood up. "Bloody pigeons."

Brian groaned as he put his weight on swollen feet, and he instinctively picked up his old police truncheon. He padded as quietly as he could into the lounge wearing red polka dot boxers and a string vest. The glow from a street light illuminated a figure in a black tracksuit and balaclava lifting his framed coin sets off the wall. The window was fully open.

"Oi! What's your game?" he shouted, causing the startled figure to drop his bag and turn around. Brian reacted like the copper he used to be and moved forward to seize the slim figure by the arm whilst raising his truncheon in a threatening gesture. The response was more forceful as the intruder slapped his weak grip aside and leaned forward with a deft headbutt that sent Brian sprawling to the floor.

Brian's head bounced off the hardwood coffee table on his way down, and he lay unconscious on the worn carpet, blood oozing from his nose, allowing his assailant to collect his haul and slip out silently back through the open window.

Brian gurgled a bit, slowly choking on his own blood and saliva. A pigeon settled on the windowsill, cooing a soft requiem in the pre-dawn half-light, its wing flaps the only send-off for the former detective sergeant of the Met's Flying Squad. Brian's beat around the streets of London had come to a sudden, violent, and lonely end. The pigeon twisted its head, listening, then hopped in and flew to the table, pecking at some crumbs in the still, pre-dawn gloom.

Mac the Ripper

On cushioned feet he floated, ankle-deep in fog along Brick Lane, making a swift left turn into a side street and out of the gaslight's dim glow. He selected his victim and followed her, not caring who she was, her occupation, social class, or ethnicity; he acted out of a deep, brooding anger, a hatred of women. The madness, the headaches, the heartburn could only be soothed with the thrill of slashing a terrified victim; her spattering blood and wide-eyed terror his elixir.

Past red brick houses, between dim streetlamp halos, he followed her swishing skirt and black bonnet as she turned into a courtyard. It had to be now. He quickened his pace, rounding the corner and then, seeing that they were alone, he rushed up behind her as she searched for a door key. Placing his hand over her mouth to suppress any cries, he wrestled her to the ground. A robotic arm moved up and down in a repetitive stabbing motion, reducing his terrified victim to a bloody mess of shredded flesh in torn clothes. Her eyes fluttered and closed, a groan escaped her throat as he stood back to admire his work.

It was all over in less than a minute, her lifeless remains dragged unceremoniously into a dark corner. Bonus points for a quick kill without any interruptions and hiding the body. After a couple of careful wipes of his butcher's knife on her dress, he was off, out of the courtyard and along the street, seeking the shadows and blending into the night...

Wide-eyed and heart pounding, Tom stared at the screen, gripped by an incredible adrenaline rush. He'd got a high score!

"Tom! Your dinner's ready! Come downstairs now!"

His concentration broken, Tom pulled himself away from the world of graphic 3D images. Best not annoy her. He sent a quick email to his friends: *Reached level four with high score!* ...then saved and shut down.

Tom got up from his desk and opened the hatch in the floor of his loft bedroom and fed down the retractable aluminium ladder, making a reversed descent in a well-practised manoeuvre. He was happy to have the loft room, as it provided much-needed sanctuary and privacy for the hours he spent immersed in social media and computer gaming.

"I hope you've been doing your homework and not playing those silly computer games. Your teacher, that nice Mrs Patel, said you were falling behind."

"Yes, Mum, I've done my homework," Tom casually lied, sitting at his usual place at the kitchen table.

"Here, love, look at this in *The Standard*." Tom's dad, Billy, looked over the top of his upright tabloid.

"What is it?" Mel drawled, as she dished up the chicken Kievs with oven chips and baked beans.

"Look, there's been a murder not far from here. 'Woman Slain in Frenzied Knife Attack' it says."

She took the paper off him and read. "Oh yes, and right next to my hairdressers. Wonder if I knew her, poor cow."

"There won't be any details for a few days," Billy offered, as if an expert in these matters. "The police have got to do their forensics thing and interview any witnesses, and then tell the victim's family before they go public. I'll ask around down the bookies tomorrow."

"Oh, you will, will you? Any excuse to throw our money away! You'd be better off going to the DIY place to buy some shelves and put them up in the spare bedroom. Do something useful on your day off..."

He lifted his newspaper again and tuned out from her nagging. She plonked the plates on the table and gazed out of the kitchen window to their brick-walled yard, as night descended on Whitechapel.

"Makes you wonder who's out there," she said as they settled down to eat.

The next morning, Tom went to school, Mel went to work, and Billy wandered off to find out what he could about the brutal murder so close to home. The man behind the counter in the corner shop said he'd heard that it was a young Bangladeshi woman, not from his community, mind, who'd had her throat slashed and body dismembered, in a recreation of the 1888 Jack the Ripper murders. Not only that, but it took place in the same courtyard where one of the original murders had taken place, over a hundred and thirty years ago. He told Billy that the most detailed report was in *The Times* and sold him a copy with a sly wink to the other man in the shop. Billy reluctantly parted with the money - he'd become used to picking up a free copy of *The Standard* from outside The Underground.

Billy MacMullen had lived in the East End all his life and had seen a lot of change. The new wave of immigrant settlers were Indians and Bangladeshis, the latter predominantly Muslims. An old Christian church had been converted into a mosque, with a neon-lit minaret now dominating Brick Lane. The Eastern European Jews and French Huguenots had dissipated into the grey, misty air over the years, to be replaced with Irish and Commonwealth settlers. He stopped to look at an estate agent window. The next stage, if the estate agents had their way, would be to gentrify the area and sell tiny flat conversions to eager City workers.

"Progress, they call it," Billy muttered under his breath. "But with property prices creeping up, I could sell up and join my mates in Essex." He pushed through the door of the White Hart and ordered his first pint of the day.

It was eleven o'clock and he was the first in. Spreading *The Times* on the counter, he thumbed straight to the murder story. Tomasz, the young Polish barman, came over to see what he was looking at.

"A young woman has been murdered near here," Billy said, screwing up his eyes to read the small print size in the posh newspaper.

"Oh yes? Who was she?" Tomasz poured a pint of foaming ale and plonked it on the bar towel in front of him. It was happy hour for pensioners, and Mac Senior had previously shown his bus pass as proof of his qualification to the otherwise unfazed barman. He had stopped work early with bad feet and was sensitive to the fact that he looked a bit young to be retired, his brown hair only just showing signs of giving way to grey.

"It says she was a young woman from the Indian or Bangladeshi community, wearing a blue, patterned sari. Victim of a sustained and vicious knife attack that has the MO of the original Jack the Ripper murders."

"What is MO?" Tomasz asked.

"Modus Oper... well, it means how it was done. It's a copycat murder, in effect." Billy took a mouthful of ale and wiped the froth from his mouth with the back of his hand.

"What have cats got to do with it?" Tomasz asked.

"It's just a saying, you know, how we say things. "Copycat" means it's been copied in the exact same way. You see, in Queen Victoria's time, there were five horrific murders of women in the streets around here. Grisly murders.

Tomasz raised an eyebrow and asked, "When was that?"

Billy frowned at the small print again. "1888, it says here. In fact, one victim left this very pub just before she met her end in a dark alley." Billy paused for dramatic effect, but Tomasz had his back to him. "The paper says this latest murder was done in exactly the same way. Get it? Somebody's pretending to be Jack the Ripper. It could be someone who frequents this very pub."

Tomasz busied himself, with a concerned look on his face now.

Billy went on, his eyes scrunched over the paper, "And some people think the original killer was a Polish immigrant called Aaron Kosminski, so you'd better get your alibi straight."

"... Or the artist Walter Sickert." A hand fell on Billy's shoulder, which made him jump.

"Oh, it's you, Don!" Billy said, turning to face his grey-haired friend.

"I saw a TV documentary on the Jack the Ripper suspects and there's an American artist who painted a picture in 1888 called, *Jack the Ripper's Bedroom*. Now there's this famous novelist, a woman, saying she's convinced he was yer man," Don said, pointing to the pump handle of his favourite beer. The hovering barman nodded and proceeded to pull a frothy pint.

"Patricia Cornwell," said another customer at the bar. "I watched that."

Don took his place on a barstool next to Billy. "Sounds about right."

"Well, whoever it was, it seems that his ghost is back and is at it again. Have you read this?" Billy showed the newspaper report to his friend and ordered him a drink.

After school, Tom and his mates went to the place that everyone was talking about, but it was cordoned off with yellow tape and a white tent was covering the murder scene. They were fascinated by the idea that the grisly computer game that they were all playing had suddenly come to life with this new and real murder. In the sanctuary of their bedrooms, the competition to get the high score through five increasingly difficult levels was intense, each replicating one of the original gruesome Whitechapel murders, with authentic Victorian settings. They split up and headed to their homes to get online.

"It's just a routine enquiry, sir," said the scruffy constable. Billy was unfazed as he answered questions. He'd been at home with his wife and son. Yes, she could vouch for him.

"The thing is, Mr MacMullen, this isn't an entirely random enquiry. I note that you have a record for grievous bodily harm from a few years back..."

"Whoa, let me stop you there! That was just a fight outside a pub, it was a one-off!" Billy was affronted.

"Yeah, well, you did strike a woman, a one... Gillian Smith... and a witness said you, and I quote, 'he had blind rage in his... erm, your eyes'."

"Well, wouldn't you if you'd just had your pocket picked? She took my wallet, and I had a hell of a job getting it back. The law turned up after the event, when she'd started playing the victim. It don't mean nuffink."

"All the same, you and your wife - Melanie is it? - will both have to come in for questioning."

After the last restaurant closed on Brick Lane at 11.30, the staff were allowed to leave after clearing up. Many lived in crowded flats above the shops, but others took to the streets, glancing warily up and down as they slipped into the night.

He was hiding in a doorway, waiting. She said goodnight and left the restaurant, walking along Hanbury Street, away from the lights of Brick Lane. On clicking heels, with her coat tightly wrapped against the chilly night air, she crossed over the road and went round the corner into the dimly lit Wilkes Street, popular with film crews because of its authentic Victorian look.

He moved off and followed her, ducking into an alley or doorway when anyone passed by. She turned off into a quiet back alley between two rows of workers' cottages and he quickly followed, closing in on his quarry.

"Billy! I think that fox is in the bins again!" Mel shouted through the open kitchen door to the living room. Billy stirred himself from the sofa and moved to the back door, unlocking it, and popped his head round the corner into the cool night air. He froze in alarm at the sight before him. In the corner of their yard, next to the open back gate, a man and a woman were struggling. Billy saw a large carving knife in the man's hand as the man turned to face him, black eyes gleaming from beneath a white-turbaned head. He was standing over a cowering, gasping woman, whose scarf had been dragged back off her long, black hair in the scuffle. For what was probably only a few seconds, there was a silent standoff, a scene frozen in time, like in a Walter Sickert painting.

"Oi! What's going on there?" Billy shouted, as he stepped into the backyard. This instinctive movement to defend his property was enough to put off the assailant, who slashed at the woman in rage, causing her to fall back with a cry of pain and clatter into the bins as he fled through the open gate into the dark alley, running silently on rubber-soled trainers.

Billy called Mel and together they went to the woman's aid. Blood was running down her cheek from a deep cut, but apart from that, she appeared unhurt. Tom appeared on the scene, having reluctantly left his game console to see what all the noise was about. They took her into the kitchen, sat her down, and called the police.

Detective Inspector Julie Covington stood in the centre of the cramped living room, eyeing their collection of pictures and ornaments with mild disdain, whilst directing questions at the three members of the MacMullen family. A rush of activity was going on behind her in the tiny, terraced house as the emergency services swung into action. The young woman was being consoled and treated by paramedics, but she was too shocked to talk. Though her wound would need further attention, she was able to walk out to a waiting ambulance, wrapped in a grey blanket.

Billy couldn't wait to have his say on the day's events: "Only a few hours ago you were questioning me as a suspect! It was going to be, 'Mac the Ripper' in the papers. And the real

Ripper ends up attacking a woman in my own backyard! That's ironical, that is."

"Alright, Mr MacMullen, you were one of many local people that we questioned. You were never a suspect." DI Covington was used to dealing with prickly characters living on the fringes of the law.

Billy eventually calmed down and gave a description of the man. "He was definitely Indian with a turban, tall and well-built, with black, piercing eyes and a black, pointy beard with a moustache curled up at the edges. Oh, and he wore white trainers." Billy grinned as a detective sergeant ran out of the room to circulate the description to his colleagues.

Tom was fascinated that DI Covington was scribbling notes in a notebook. "Why are you writing notes? Shouldn't you voice-record it or type into a tablet?"

"I'll ask the questions, if you don't mind!" she snapped, her glare silencing the curious teenager.

"Right, I think I have enough for tonight. Thank you for your intervention, Mr MacMullen, you almost certainly saved that young woman's life. I'd like you to come to the station in the morning to give us a photofit portrait of the assailant, and I'd ask you all not to talk to the media as the suspect is still at large. Goodnight."

Billy saw her to the door and asked, "Do you think the victim was from the Bangladeshi community, like the first one?"

The inspector shrugged and said nothing. Her radio crackled to life: "Ma'am, we've just apprehended a suspect matching the witness's description, just off Brick Lane..."

She jumped into a car and sped off, the blue lights flashing in the dark night.

"Did you hear that?" Billy shouted triumphantly, "They've caught him down Brick Lane!"

"Well, that's a cause for celebration," Mel said, "I'll put the kettle on."

"Wow! With all the excitement I don't think any of us will be getting to sleep for a while," said Billy.

Tom was full of admiration for his dad. "I can't believe you took on the Ripper, Dad! Wicked!" He paced the tiny room, high on an adrenalin buzz. "It's a double whammy, Dad! You helped catch the Ripper and I got the high score on the *Jack the Ripper* game!"

Mel entered carrying a tea tray and admonished him. "You're supposed to be doing your homework up there, not playing computer games!"

After some reflection, Billy was ready to share his theory. "As I see it, it's the Curry House Wars."

Mel started to choke on her biscuit. "Billy, you can't say that!" She glanced over to where her innocent and easily influenced son was sitting in silence, oblivious to the fact that he was gearing up for another evening of virtual violence.

"Well, the perpetrator comes from the Indian Sikh community, who control the Brick Lane Indian restaurant business. His victims are from the Bangladeshi community, who have muscled into the Brick Lane area, setting up restaurants and undercutting the more established businesses..."

Mel cut him off. "Oh come on, Billy, you don't know that. Just like they didn't know about Jack the bleedin' Ripper. It could have been anyone wearing a turban as a disguise. Better keep your thoughts to yourself until the police have questioned him. They can do all that DNA-matching stuff these days. If you ask me, it's got very creepy living round here with someone running around imitating those horrible murders. History belongs in history books. I hope that's the end of it."

"The original Ripper murders are still unsolved, love. So, the book is still open. There's a final chapter still to be written." He picked up his newspaper with a smirk of satisfaction at his clever conclusion.

"Dad," Tom said. "Do you think they'll put one of them blue plaques outside our house? You know, the ones for famous people?"

Mel laughed, "Saying what exactly?"

Tom put his mug of tea down and sat forward with a serious expression. "It could say: 'Here Lives Mac the Ripper-Catcher'."

Whilst Mel snorted her derision, Billy looked at his son with admiration.

"Yeah, it has a ring to it: 'Mac the Ripper-Catcher'. I can't wait to get down the White Hart tomorrow and tell the lads."

Tom had ideas of his own and quietly retired to his room. It may have been two in the morning, but he fired up his computer and loaded the game. The night's events had given him an idea on how to avoid the long arm of the law in level five. Jack the Ripper would once again murder and evade capture, the legend would live on, and Tom would be crowned game champion.

The Seesaw Sea of Fate

Red is supposed to make you thirsty, so say the psychologists, Stephen Joyce thought, as he surveyed the stained red carpet and matching flock wallpaper on the walls of the pub. Old and dirty, it had an unloved look about it. The walls between the cream, chipped sash windows had framed prints of scenes from old London. The one nearest him had a Victorian gent in a top hat strolling along a pavement with a parasol-touting lady on his arm. Glancing at his phone, he checked the time again - a quarter past two. Sean was late.

It was Sean who had proposed that they meet up for a pub crawl for Stephen's birthday. They'd worked together from the late 80s to the mid-90s on Fleet Street when Stephen was a young reporter and Sean Malone a printer in the dungeons of Associated Newspapers.

By the mid-90s, the golden age of newspaper publishing on Fleet Street had come to an end, with Associated moving west to Kensington as the financial sector spread its tentacles outwards from the City to meet the legal firms clustered around the Inner Temple, squeezing out the wheezing, alcoholic newspaper men. The end of an era. Both Stephen and Sean left the company at that time and moved on to pastures new in digital media. They had kept in touch, but now only met up a couple of times a year as their lives had moved in different directions.

Stephen was in one of his favourite City pubs, the Fitzroy Tavern on Charlotte Street in the heart of Fitzrovia, once the bohemian centre of literary inspiration from the romantic poets right through to twentieth-century figures including Dylan Thomas, George Orwell, and Anthony Burgess. Yes, inspiration at the bottom of a pint glass. How many of the great poets and novelists of English literature had been inspired by boozy conversations and sore-headed reflection? His musings were cut short by Sean's bustling figure, accompanied by a cold draught as he burst through the side door.

"Sorry I'm late, delays on the Northern Line, don't ya know? Anyway, great to see yer, mate, and happy birthday!" He shook Stephen firmly by the hand. "What're yer havin'?" Sean pulled off his coat, throwing it beside Stephen, and turned to the bar.

They settled into the corner booth and started to chat like old friends with some catching up to do. Now, in 2015, both were in their mid-forties, and the once-timeless pleasure of sitting in pubs had ebbed but was now briefly revived as they sipped on their pints, enjoying the banter. Sean's Irish accent was as strong as ever, despite having lived in London for over twenty years. "Oi've been workin' for a printin' firm up in Kilburn, not far from my digs. It ain't as well paid as Associated, but it's walking distance from where I live, and has the best pubs in London." He took a long draught from his pint of Guinness. "What've yer been up to?"

Stephen described his ups and downs. He had left Associated after completing his training as a news reporter and went to work for Reuters News Agency. This had enabled him to travel to some of the worst war zones on earth - Bosnia, Somalia, Iraq, and Afghanistan. He had lived in tents, army barracks, and neglected hotel rooms, reporting on the lives of the victims of war, soldiers in the field, as well as on the conflicts themselves. "Wars used to be territorial disputes or aggressive conquest, until Iraq and Afghanistan."

"Oh yeah? Why were they different?" Sean asked.

"Those were the wars on terror; the West's revenge against the Islamic terror attacks. Although the history of the colonial powers tinkering in the Middle East goes way back to the nineteenth century."

"So, pr'haps it's just a continuation of that?" Sean offered with a shrug, not really bothered.

Stephen had come to understand the utter futility of these stage-managed conflicts, and seen that the shattered lives, poverty, and despair was absent from the sterile war rooms in London and Washington. He now worked as a home-based freelance feature writer, from his cluttered office in a cosy flat in Islington. He had also found the time to get married to his fellow reporter, Julia, and they had a six-year-old son, James.

"So, what's the plan?" Stephen asked his friend. "Oi taught we'd go round the pubs in this area, cut through Soho, and end up in the Tattershall Castle - y'know, the pub boat on the river at the Embankment." He grinned as he raised his glass with a mischievous twinkle in his eye.

"Very convenient for the Northern Line," Stephen replied with a snort and a wink. "Oh yeah, I can recall many a boozy night on the floating pub on the river - good shout!" They clinked glasses in a toast to old times. "We'll grab a bite to eat as we weave our way through Chinatown."

"Drink up, let's move on," Sean said as he downed his pint and grabbed his coat. Outside, they turned north up Charlotte Street, crossing over the road and round the corner into Charlotte Place and into the Duke of York. "Ahh, one of my favourite pubs," Stephen said, "A decent pint of bitter and the place where Anthony Burgess was alleged to have found inspiration for *A Clockwork Orange*, following an altercation with some knife-wielding thugs."

They found some elbow room at the bar and stood supping their pints. "Have you tried writing a book yerself?" Sean inquired.

"Well, actually, I have copious notes from my war correspondent days and it's in the back of my mind to write up an account of it. But I can't separate the politics from what happened on the ground. War is what happens when the political process breaks down. Getting stuck on the motives and machinations of self-serving political leaders like Bush and Blair kind of puts me off from starting it."

They drank quietly for a couple of minutes. "Come on, let's move on," Stephen added, standing. They wandered down Rathbone Street to the Marquis of Granby. Entering the faded grandeur of the old pub, they sat beneath pictures of prize fighters adorning the walls.

Sean said, "Now it's my turn to tell you something about this pub. It was here that the rules of boxing were first thought up by the Marquis of Queensbury and his high society friends. A gentlemen's sport, fought by poor men for money."

Stephen wasn't to be outdone and added, "Literary figures also drank here, including Eric Blair, who wrote as George Orwell. He worked for the BBC, just round the corner, during the Second World War, helping the war effort with propaganda programmes, where he no doubt got his ideas for *Animal Farm* and *1984*. This pub inspires me, Sean. To think that *1984*, one of the great English novels, may have been dreamed up in here; that Blair, or rather, Orwell, rubbed shoulders with working-class men having a pint after work, and sketched the character of Winston Smith in his mind. That TV programme *Room 101* is based on a reference in *1984*. It was the place where political prisoners, including the unfortunate Winston Smith, met their fate. A boot stamping on a human face forever was Orwell's bleak description of what happened in Room 101. The fact that they've made light entertainment out of it cracks me up."

"Never read it," Sean said with a shrug, "Although I heard that the futuristic fantasy film, *Brazil*, borrows heavily from it."

Stephen laughed. "For a printer, you don't read much!"

"The only English literature I'm interested in is the form on the horses in the Saturday paper. This is more of a sporting pub, with the pictures of boxers on the walls. You got any interest in sport?"

Stephen paid for the beers and sipped the frothy top of his pint. "Only the fortunes of Arsenal. I used to go up to the old Highbury Stadium and stand on the North Bank. Those were the days — the back four of Adams, Bould, Winterburn, Dixon, and David Seaman in goal. Those ugly buggers scared off all the attackers. No wonder Arsenal boasted the meanest defence and the most humourless manager in George Graham. I like the current manager, Arsène Wenger, but somehow, I can't summon up the enthusiasm to go to the new Emirates Stadium. I hear the ticket prices are astronomical."

"Yeah," Sean chipped in, "I only watch the horses in the bookies and the footy in the pub."

From there, they stopped in The Wheatsheaf on Rathbone Place, a narrow pub which used to be a coaching inn in days gone by. "This was the pub where Dylan Thomas met his wife-to-be, Caitlin," Stephen announced, determined to continue inflicting his literary pub facts on his old mate. "She was with another man, but Dylan chatted her up and started dating her. After a whirlwind romance, they got married and lived happily together until Dylan's early death from the demon drink."

"Sounds like a man after me own heart," Sean chuckled.

Stephen continued: "I brought Julia here for a drink one time and told her the same story about Dylan Thomas. She surprised me by reciting a few lines from his poem, *Under Milk Wood*. I can still remember it:

The only sea I saw
Was the seesaw sea
With you riding on it.
Lie down, lie easy.
Let me shipwreck in your thighs

I knew from that moment I was in love and was destined to marry her."

Sean chuckled, "So, what worked for Dylan Thomas, worked for you, p'raps at this very same table. C'mon, let's move on." He'd got the thirst for it and drained his pint in three gulps.

It was a chilly, blustery October day and it was already getting dark at four-thirty as they headed towards Oxford Street. Stephen, celebrating his forty-fourth birthday, had already had four pints to Sean's three, and was starting to rock from side to side, like a ship caught in a heavy sea swell.

"Whoops! I'm rolling on the seesaw sea!" Stephen cried as he stepped back onto the pavement as a Boris Bike sped by, splashing some rainwater onto his shoes. It was crowded with shoppers, and Stephen turned to see Sean swerving through a group of six Muslim women, veiled and clad from head to foot in black, who parted to let him through, then closed ranks after he'd passed, hurrying on their way, not replying to his, "Oops, sorry!" as he nearly barged into them.

"Bejesus, they can't even acknowledge you," he muttered under his breath, "London used to be a friendly place."

They navigated their way past black cabs and red buses to the south side of Oxford Street and headed towards Soho Square.

As they hurried down Dean Street into the heart of Soho, Stephen decided to have some fun with his friend. "You're a fine one to comment on the multicultural society - you Paddies are everywhere!"

Sean let out a loud guffaw and replied, "Come on, the Brits and the Irish are practically cousins. We're all from the same wet and windswept islands off the north coast of Europe. London's now full of those who 'tink they can bypass hundreds of years of development by coming on a rubber dingy or bunking through the Channel Tunnel just so they can get subsidised housing, and free education and healthcare. They're spoiling it for the rest of us."

"They're just the latest wave of centuries of settlers," Stephen muttered. "Who can claim to be pure British? I think I'm part Briton, Celt, and Dane."

"Then let's agree to not throw each other out!" Stephen shouted, slapping his friend on the back as the drizzle intensified.

They pushed through the door of the next pub on their journey, the Coach and Horses on Greek Street, a busy pub with an upstairs restaurant frequented by actors, actresses, playwrights, and theatre workers. Sean muscled his way to the bar and ordered the round.

Stephen reverted back to pub tour guide. "Now, let me tell you something about this pub. The journalist and barroom raconteur Jeffrey Bernard used to drink here, and it's where playwright Keith Waterhouse got his inspiration to write the play *Jeffrey Bernard Is Unwell*. It's set in this very pub, where Jeffrey wakes in the early hours of the morning and emerges from under a table to reflect on his life-long association with booze. In fact, he died from alcohol-related complications shortly after the play opened."

"Wasn't that a TV film with my hero, Peter O'Toole, in it?" Sean asked.

Stephen grinned. "Yes, it was O'Toole's last showing as well, before the demon drink also caught up with him. Like I said before. There's a strong relationship between booze and English literature."

Sean touched his glass against Stephen's and said, in a mock-sombre voice, "To the memory of the late, great Peter O'Toole, piss artist extraordinaire."

Stephen put his empty pint glass down on the bar and said, "Let's take a break from the demon booze and get something to eat. How about we go over the road into Chinatown for a Chinese?"

Sean nodded and they made their way across Shaftesbury Avenue, past the chattering theatre-goers spilling out from the matinee performances, through the archway into Chinatown, weaving along Gerrard Street and into the Four Seasons restaurant. The ground floor was full of diners, and they were ushered up a rickety, wooden staircase where they were seated at a large, round table with other recent arrivals.

"Service is rubbish, but the aromatic duck is to die for," Stephen whispered. Sean briefly scanned the menu, before Stephen leaned over and pointed to the Set Menu for Two.

"That'll do," Sean said, ordering two pints of lager from the tiny waiter.

Stephen frowned and added a bottle of mineral water to the order. He opened up a new subject: "You haven't told me if you're seeing anyone at the moment?"

"Erm, no, not at the moment. I'm between relationships," he smiled. "I had a girlfriend, Molly, until a couple of months ago. She was from County Clare and worked behind the bar in The Jolly Miller. It didn't work out - she worked long hours in the evenings and on weekends; it was impossible to go out for a date, and I got jealous of all the lads chatting her up. I bet you're loving it, being a husband and daddy."

"Yeah, it's great, it's really given me a new purpose and direction in life. You can't go on being young, free, and single forever."

"Don't know about that," Sean said, "London's the place to be if you're single. There's plenty of distractions here."

They laughed and joked as they rolled up their duck pancakes, then tucked into bowls of fried rice and things swimming in monosodium glutamate. Sean insisted on paying as it was Stephen's birthday and he had invited him out.

"You're a bad lad, Sean, but it's good to see you again. I remember our drinking days around Fleet Street and Blackfriars. We were young then; we worked hard and played hard, spending whatever we earned in the pubs. This is a timely reminder that it's all still here. Life goes on; it's just that the punters get younger. Let's head on to that pub next to Charing Cross Station and then down the alleyway to the Embankment and onto the Tattershall Castle."

Sean took his opportunity to say what was on his mind. "Steve, you couldn't help me out, could yer? I hate to ask, but I need a job - do you have any contacts in the production side of things?"

Stephen eyed him cautiously, rather feeling that he'd been ambushed. The alcohol was making him slow at engaging his brain to think of a reply. "I can't think of anything offhand. Let me give it some thought over the next few days."

There was a slightly awkward and embarrassing silence, broken by Sean. "Yeah, of course, sorry to ask, but yer know how it is."

"No problem, mate, that's what friends are for. I'll help if I can." Stephen put his arm around his friend's shoulder in a brief hug, then manfully disengaged as they strode on.

They walked out into the well-lit, narrow street and turned their coat collars up against the wind and rain. Theatre-goers hurried by for the evening performance, smartly dressed in dinner jackets or long dresses, on a special night out.

They returned to small talk about the people they'd worked with and the nights out they'd had. Time had changed things; the intervening years had taken them in different directions with differing fortunes. The excitement and energy of their youth had given way to the more circumspect and practical view of middle age.

"For one night only!" a neon sign shouted above a theatre entrance. Stephen pointed to it and said, "One night only for me, my friend - I hardly get out these days. I'm really enjoying this nostalgic stagger across London!"

The Tattershall Castle swayed gently at its mooring next to the Embankment riverside walk. The old iron boat had been colourfully painted in blue and yellow, and they had to duck their heads as they went below deck to the cosy bar. It gave the sense of being somewhere away from the city, the illusion of travelling to faraway places. London was the start and end point for many journeys over the ages. They were both pretty drunk by now and Stephen in particular was feeling the effect. "I think this'll be my last, I'm as pissed as the proverbial newt."

Sean eyed up some attractive office workers giggling across the bar as they moved to a standing-only table. "I feel the sudden need for a fag," he said.

"You haven't smoked at all this evening, I thought you'd given up," Stephen said.

"Ah well, yer know, after a few pints I still get the urge. I'll just go up on deck for a quick smoke. See you in a bit."

Stephen smiled as his friend bounced off the wood panels, following an equally drunk woman up the stairs. He fished his mobile phone out of his coat pocket and checked his messages, then replied to a text from his wife. He was distracted by shouts, screams, followed by a splash coming from up on deck. Curious drinkers responded by running up the stairs. Stephen followed. A distraught, inebriated woman was pointing into the river, and Stephen saw his friend Sean bobbing up and down, his arms flailing as he struggled to keep his head above the murky water of the Thames. Stephen ran along the deck and pulled a plastic life ring from the railing, throwing it to his friend. "Here! Grab hold of this!"

They managed to coax him around the bow of the boat and hauled him out onto the pontoon. "Are you alright, mate? What happened?" Stephen was sobering up fast in the cool night air. Sean looked up at him and rolled over, vomiting brown river water mixed with Chinese noodles. "Come on, let's get you home." Stephen managed to get him to his feet and got him to put his coat on - at least that was dry. "We'd better get a taxi back to my place."

They earned a round of applause and rowdy shouts of encouragement from the partying office workers. Sean just groaned and submitted to his friend dragging him up the gang plank.

At Stephen's flat, Sean was briefly introduced to a shocked Julia before being guided to the shower. Stephen explained what had happened and sorted out some old clothes to give to his friend. With a hot mug of coffee cradled in his hands, Sean sheepishly apologised to Julia. She smiled and fussed, blaming her wayward husband for what she assumed was a drunken prank that had got out of hand.

"Come on Sean, tell us what happened, and get me out of jail!" Stephen wailed.

Sean gulped a mouthful of warm coffee and said, "Stephen's not to blame, Julia. In fact, he wasn't even there. I was on the top deck, flirting with a woman who I'd just bummed a fag off. Well, I leaned backwards on the railing, posing, and it opened like a gate, and before I knew it, I was falling down into the river."

"Oh my God! You must have been terrified!" Julia said, shocked.

"Yeah, my life flashed before me, and it wasn't a pretty sight. Anyway, now I know what the Thames tastes like, and I won't be bottling it."

Stephen suddenly sprung to life, "That's it! I think I've got a job for you, Sean." He turned to his wife. "Honey, you remember your friend who works for the bottled water company?"

"Yes, you mean Lucy at the Essex Spring Water Company... what about her?"

"Well, she said they were looking for someone to organise their labels and publicity leaflets. Well, young Sean here is a publishing guru, a veritable design wizard, and he's looking for a new job. It could be a perfect match!"

Sean brightened up and managed a smile, "Wow, a job reference is almost worth taking a swim in the Thames for. That could really help, Julia. I've done plenty of labels and leaflets."

Julia smiled and offered Sean a biscuit. "Then email me your CV and I'll make the introduction."

Sean sat back and beamed like a leprechaun from the Emerald Isle. "Good contacts, a recommendation, and the luck of the Irish - that's the way to get a job in this kaleidoscopic revolving-door city. As Dylan Thomas might've said, it's the seesaw sea of fate. Any more coffee going?"

Geraniums

"Come and have a look at this."

I looked up from reading the tag on a geranium plant in the greenhouse extension of the garden centre, just as the sunlight burst out from behind a dark cloud. Momentarily disoriented, I raised my hand to shield my eyes. "Just coming, dear."

I navigated past some luxurious terracotta pot plants - some practically leaping out in an exuberant celebration of life. Funny how they never grow like that in your own garden, I thought. Maggie was holding up a green canvas gardening apron with three generous pockets at the front.

"This would be perfect for you, darling," she beamed. It was her mission to get me to take a more active interest in the gardeners' world that she'd created in and around our house. I'd recently retired and was still in the shocked and numb phase as my mind slowly adjusted to having nothing much to do.

"You know I don't look good in green, dear," I replied, as I gazed idly beyond her at the huge palm trees lined against the far wall. A man in a white robe moved behind Maggie and bent down to pick up the same item. She followed the line of my gaze and took a half-step away from the Middle Eastern-looking man, dark-skinned with the custom black beard and leather sandals, as we both rather rudely stared at him. He looked up at me and smiled, perhaps used to and enjoying the stares, and swiftly bent down to pick up the remaining gardener's pinnies. As he folded them, his black eyes fixed on the apron Maggie was holding, and she reacted by hugging it close against her.

"I'm getting this one," she announced, as she grabbed my arm and dragged me away from the man. We picked up some gardening tools on our way to the checkout. The Middle Eastern man soon appeared in the queue opposite us, pushing a trolley loaded with fertiliser, some tools, fencing materials and the three canvas pinnies on top.

"Don't stare, George," she admonished, as our turn came. We made our way to our car, and after I'd taken my time loading everything up, the white-robed man appeared and made his way to his vehicle. As he approached the gunmetal-grey people carrier with darkened windows, the side door slid open for him. He loaded up his purchases and jumped in the front passenger seat. I got behind the wheel and started up my engine - Maggie was rooting around in her bag and hadn't noticed my line of gaze.

As his vehicle joined the queue of cars waiting to exit the car park, I joined behind it. Leaving the car park, I turned left and followed it.

"Where are you going?" Maggie cried.

"I thought we could have a nice pub Sunday lunch, as we haven't bought anything perishable?"

She paused as if thinking about kitchen matters. "Oh, alright. I haven't got anything out the freezer, and we've got some leftovers for this evening." She smiled warmly and hugged my arm.

We continued as the grey vehicle wound through the side streets, and finally pulled onto the driveway of a semi-detached house on the opposite side of town to where we lived. I slowed down and looked over to see the house number.

"What are you looking at?" she demanded.

"Oh, erm, just trying to remember if I've been here before." I immediately regretted this as she continued to press me.

"Why would you have been here before? We don't know anyone who lives in this street."

"No, I think I dropped someone from work around here once, but not this street. A new guy called Alan."

Now she was suspicious. "Oh really? You've never mentioned dropping anyone home, or someone at work called Alan to me before."

"I had those leaving drinks, remember? The one you didn't come to because you had a headache? I used the excuse of having to drive so I wouldn't have to hang around too long. I withdrew quietly with my engraved clock shortly after the speeches. The new guy asked me for a lift ... oh, here we are." I pulled into the car park of an old, oak-beamed pub, The Quiet Man.

"An appropriately named pub, George," she said in her I'm-not-sure-I-believe-you voice. "You always were the quiet one."

I smiled as I unbuckled, happy to deflect her forensic mind onto a new strand. "That's our natural division of labour, dear - you do the pontificating, and I quietly keep us steering a steady course."

We ordered and sat on a wooden picnic bench in the immaculate garden. A willow tree bowed towards a stream that fed, some miles away, into the mighty River Thames, the silent witness of human settlement in this part of the country going back thousands of years. A swan floated by to complete the idyllic scene.

My mind dwelt resolutely on matters as opaque as the dark waters that had witnessed battles and murders aplenty, including the recent crop of suicide bombings in nearby London; often on bridges or close to the banks of the impassive river, its muddy flow never flinching, but silently accepting the unfortunate victims of circumstance, folding them in and sucking them down into the cold embrace of Old Father Thames. It was only a year since the London terror bombings on public transport of July 2007, in which fifty-two innocent souls lost their lives. The memory was still raw

I'd found a new hobby. I was determined to investigate the garden centre man, as I felt something wasn't quite right. But how do you conduct a DIY investigation with no experience of police work? My previous life as a market research manager had equipped me well for information-gathering, and I had an encyclopaedic knowledge of sources.

When Maggie had held up the green canvas apron to show me in the garden centre that day, I'd greeted it with a sinking feeling, as I imagined myself forever kneeling next to the flower beds with trowels and forks protruding from my handily placed pockets.

That vision soon changed when I saw the man standing behind her, holding up the apron and pressing it to his belly with a smile. He looped the strap over his head and thrust his fists into the generous pockets to get an idea of their capacity. Capacity for what? Was I being a hysterical Englishman, a victim of the intentions of terrorists who want to spread, well, terror amongst a passive, pampered population? It was barely a year since the awful events of July 2007, the terrorist attacks that the papers had branded London's 9/11.

"Lambs waiting to be slaughtered," I muttered as I started working through a keywords search on my laptop.

"What did you say, dear?" Maggie called from the kitchen.

"Oh, just thinking out loud. I'm searching for gardening ideas." Little white lies were woven into the very fabric of our marriage, like a tapestry with patches that had been picked at, rendering elements unknown. She did it too, so why should I feel guilty?

Perhaps our mystery man was just a keen gardener. Maybe that was it - I could pose as a market researcher to ask questions on gardening, admitting, if pressed, that the lead had been passed on by Homebase. Sorry for the intrusion, etc. I set about designing a bogus questionnaire. No need to bother the wife.

Geraniums, red and wild, once planted with loving care, now battled with the uncut grass that was encroaching on the borders in Mr Abdul Rashid's front garden. I'd done my best to alter my appearance in the five days since my visit to the garden centre: haircut, shave, different glasses, and my old work clothes of trousers, white shirt, tie, jacket, and black leather shoes. I rang the doorbell and stepped back, noting the peeling white paint on the wood and glass porch.

"Hello, can I help you?" A man's face protruded through a narrow crack in the door. He looked very similar to the man from the garden centre.

"Good morning, sir. My name is Brendan, and I'm conducting a survey on behalf of a retail client for a market research company. Could you spare a few minutes of your time?"

He opened the door a bit wider and stood before me in a cream robe, scratching his black beard as he regarded me with dark, almost black, eyes. "Is this a random house call?" he asked.

"Not exactly," I replied, "it's a lead from the local Homebase store. Someone from this address shopped there recently, and I'm conducting a survey of home furnishings and gardening. May I come in for a few minutes?"

He hesitated before stepping back and holding the door open for me. I walked into the hallway and waited for my host. As he shuffled past me, I noted that he was shorter than both me and the man I'd followed from the garden centre. His brother, perhaps?

He turned and said, "May I see your ID please, Mr... erm?"

"Oliver. Yes, of course, here it is." I handed him my fake ID card.

He scrutinised it before handing it back. "Tea, Mr Oliver?"

"Yes please. Milk, no sugar."

He led me to the rear lounge that backed onto the garden. Left alone, I leafed through some magazines that included British and Middle Eastern current affairs, some with graphic pictures of war zone victims with appalling injuries. I stood and moved gingerly through the deep, cream shag carpet towards the patio doors. An overgrown and foreboding garden mocked a lean-to transparent greenhouse that was positively bulging with bags of fertiliser and various gardening implements, including shears and what looked like long knives or machetes. Hearing movement, I scurried back to my seat.

"So, what questions would you like to ask me, Mr Oliver?" He placed a tray with two teacups and saucers on the coffee table.

"Right, let's get started." I was on safe ground, as I knew how to administer a questionnaire. "Firstly, may I have your name?" Pen poised over a form, I met his stare.

With a smile he replied, "I am Abdul Rashid."

May I ask, how long have you lived in this property?"

"Six months."

"And how often do you tend to the garden?"

"Not at all. My wife waters it when it's dry, but as you can see, it hasn't been mowed or the flowers tended to yet." He smiled and sipped his drink.

"May I ask what gardening items you purchased recently from Homebase?"

"It wasn't me who visited Homebase," he said.

"Was it another member of the household?" I persisted.

"You could say that. It was my brother, Mohammed. He's staying with us for a short while."

"And what did he buy?"

I locked eyes on Abdul Rashid and tried my best not to blink. After what seemed like an age, he smiled and replied. "Some planting compost and some tools for the garden. He has promised to get out there and sort it out for me."

"Thank you." I ticked a box and continued to run through my short survey, finally getting to the personal details section.

"Can I ask which of these age groups you are in?" Making a considered guess I prompted, 31 to 40, or 41 to 50?"

"The first," he tersely replied.

"And how long have you been living in the UK?"

He stood up and challenged me in a forceful manner. "Surely that isn't a question! Show me where that's written!"

I duly complied and showed him the question on my purpose-made questionnaire. He glanced at the bogus name of my market research company.

"It's just so the client company, in this case Homebase, can build up a profile…"

"But I'm not their customer!" he shouted, then checked himself and lowered his voice. A woman scurried past the doorway into the kitchen. "I'm sorry, Mr Oliver, for raising my voice. I've told you that I'm not the gardener, nor the store customer, so you're talking to the wrong person. And now, you've taken up enough of my time. Thank you." He stood with his outstretched arm and open palm pointing towards the hallway.

"That's fine, Mr Rashid. Thank you for your time." I beat a hasty retreat, walking to the next road where I'd left my car, out of sight of the house.

Once home, I surprised Maggie by pouring myself a large gin and tonic.

"Starting early, are we?" she asked, arching her eyebrows.

"Minor road rage incident," I lied. "Something and nothing. Will you join me?"

"Don't mind if I do," she said cheerfully. We sat in our cushioned rattan chairs in the conservatory, slipping into familiar small talk, enjoying the late afternoon sunshine.

The next morning, I couldn't wait to fire up the laptop and start writing a report based on my observations and the answers to the survey. In truth, I was slightly missing my old job, and this was sort of a substitute. I wrote my account in as objective and factual manner as I could, but later drew some subjective "what-if" assumptions. Reading them back, they seemed rather far-fetched, although perhaps not in the current climate of random terrorist incidents and the fear they engendered:

- Two Muslim men and a woman living in a house in Walton-on-Thames, close to London, in 2008
- The man interviewed, Mr Adbul Rashid, appears to be of Middle Eastern origin
- The Rashid couple have been there for six months – his brother, Mohammed, is a recent visitor
- Mohammed bought fertiliser, compost, a gardening apron and tools despite there being no evidence of an interest in gardening
- There were shears, knives, and machetes in their greenhouse
- Conclusion: There are some ingredients for making a bomb and sharp objects that could be used for committing violent acts from members of a high-risk ethnic and religious group

I stood up and gazed at our cat stalking a piece of paper blowing across the garden. Was I being too melodramatic? Was I guilty of prejudicial racial and religious profiling? Had I seen too many ugly news reports and was now jittery after years of random and terrifying acts of violence? Terrorism does work. It leaves the mark of fear on a population, flicking a primitive switch that says 'beware - danger!' I resolved to go to the police station the following morning with my report. Let them act on it or ignore it. They're the experts.

"Fish fingers and oven chips for tea, dear?" Maggie shouted from the kitchen.

"Yes, that's fine. Good, old-fashioned comfort food," I replied.

I was slightly miffed by the oh-no-here-we-go-again attitude of the doleful desk sergeant. He listened with practiced patience and took my printed report, saying someone would ring me. They didn't. Two weeks had passed, and the duly anointed day of our annual trip to the West End to see a show had arrived.

"You know, in a secular society this is a kind of quasi-religious pilgrimage," I shouted as Maggie readied herself.

"What are you on about?" she shouted back. "Have you been on the gin already?"

"I mean, we're now living in an advanced Western capitalist and increasingly secular state where money is worshipped, and wealth is idolised, and the achievements of mankind in terms of scientific discovery and technology have made the old religions pretty much redundant. We're now going to our temple to pay homage to the gods of opulence and cultural identity, to bow down before Miss Saigon, as it were …"

"You *have* been on the gin, haven't you? Stop wittering on and zip up my dress. The minicab will be here soon."

We alighted from our train and walked from Waterloo Station down to the South Bank and along the promenade, climbing the stone steps to Westminster Bridge.

"Oh look, they've put in metal railings between the road and pavement," Maggie said, pointing.

"Ah yes, the anti-terror barriers, designed to stop pedestrians being mown down in what they refer to as "low-tech" attacks. Rather ugly, don't you think?" I replied.

We stopped halfway across the bridge to admire the Houses of Parliament; its sandstone blocks glowing orange in the early evening sun. I looked down into the brown, swirling waters of the Thames as Maggie fished around in her bag for her mobile. She posed me for a snap, looking dapper in my evening suit, and we stopped a passerby to take one of the two of us. Maggie looked resplendent in her fake fur-lined camel coat, her blonde curls dancing merrily in the breeze. As I framed another picture, I noticed people shouting and running in the background. I clicked her smile and quickly changed the setting to video. Something serious was going on at the entrance to Westminster Tube station.

"Where are you going, dear?" Maggie asked, as I walked past her towards the commotion, holding her phone in front of me. People were running, towards us and past us, fear and anxiety etched on their faces. Maggie followed and pulled at my sleeve to stop me.

A flash of light was followed a nano-second later by a loud explosion that shook the bridge under our feet, causing us to stagger. I put my arm around Maggie, and we instinctively crouched by the stone wall as bits of masonry and assorted debris rained down on us. A large, black cloud billowed over the Underground station entrance, with screams and shouts providing a chilling soundtrack. My ears were ringing, and I felt dazed. I looked at Maggie to check that she was alright and we slumped into a sitting position as I held her tightly around her shoulders, trying to stay calm.

Flower petals settled on us, and I picked one up. I was in a surreal dream of odd shapes and noises, an unfamiliar world where time has been slowed down and oddly distorted.

"Pelargoniums," I slurred, hardly hearing myself over the ringing in my ears. "We call them geraniums; a single, red flowering plant... native to South Africa... popularised by US President Thomas Jefferson in the eighteenth century..."

Maggie looked at me with a combination of shock, annoyance, and concern in her blue eyes. Picture postcards of London scenes and debris from a nearby kiosk rained down like confetti. One, singed at the edges, fluttered into her lap. Tower Bridge by moonlight. Someone then tripped over my outstretched foot and stumbled, falling to their hands and knees.

"Oh, sorry, let me help you," I reacted instinctively, awkwardly trying to get up, like a drunk being buffeted on a fast train. He was on his feet before me. I stood, swaying, blinking, and rubbing ash from my eyes. I was face to face with… a black-bearded black eyed Middle Eastern man with a familial likeness to Abdul Rashid - surely his brother, Mohammed. He was wearing the now-familiar green canvas gardening apron over a long, black robe. The pockets were empty. One of his eyes was closed and the side of his face was blackened, with blood running from his ear and down to his neck. He blankly regarded me for a moment, then turned and carried on his crazy zigzag walk, holding his side with one hand and reaching for the stone wall of the bridge with the other.

"Hey! He's one of them!" I croaked, waving my arms, and pointing at the stricken man. Soon, others started to repeat my cries and two police officers came running over.

"He's there — that man in a black robe with blood on his face, and he's wearing a gardening apron!" I shouted. A female officer looked at me with a dubious expression. They ran southwards along Westminster Bridge, following Mohammed, who had almost staggered to the end of the bridge. Soon an ambulance crew found us and shrouded us in aluminium foil, then guided us away to the other side of the cordoned-off bridge and towards the South Bank.

We were handed paper cups of tea as we sat outside McDonald's with our foil blankets wrapped around us, like turkeys awaiting the oven. A St John Ambulance man checked us over for wounds and, upon finding none, moved on to the next random passerby who'd also been in the wrong place at the wrong time.

"Always there in a crisis," I mumbled. "Cuts and bruises will heal, but the psychological damage…"

Maggie pulled a flower petal from my collar and handed it to me. "You and your bloody geraniums."

"Ah, yes, very good - bloody geraniums. Very apt."

A ripple of automatic gunfire accompanied by screams away to the west drew gasps, reminding us that the drama was still unfolding. Anxious looks and an ominous silence soon gave way to relieved chatter.

"We're destined never to see *Miss Saigon*," Maggie sighed, sipping her tea, and hugging my arm. "Remember last year when your mother got sick, and we had to rush to Dorset?"

"This one will make a better story," I remark, eyeing the activity around me of the emergency services hard at work. "They truly are Britain at her finest." She followed my line of sight and nodded.

"It might actually be safer for us to go over there - to Saigon," I add. "Their civil war was over a long time ago. I can feel a bucket list tour of South-East Asia coming on."

"If this is the new normal, then we'd better buy some flak jackets, because I'm not being put off visiting this splendid city," Maggie said, hugging my arm.

My eyes moved from her creased brow to settle on a mini tornado of sweet wrappers and plastic bottles, spinning their indifference to this carnival of suffering and sectarian hatred that I know will soon dissipate as the relentless rhythm of London life resumes its steady beat.

"Life goes on, dear, and so shall we."

Blue Sky Thinking

Donald Myers was obsessed with escaping. He was only one year into a five-year stretch for fraud and embezzlement and had it fairly cushy at Belmarsh prison in Thamesmead. It was a category A prison run by the private security firm Serco, Donald called it the Betty Ford Clinic, although no one there had checked in voluntarily. The downside was sharing a cell with a smelly thief and the tasteless sludge served up as food, but the highlight of his routine-driven existence was one hour a day in the computer room.

Having worked out how to bypass the restricted access feature to the internet, he thought it amusing that he could surf to his heart's content and save his files to the Cloud. He chuckled at the image of a white, fluffy cloud floating over the prison which his data was being stored in, floating free in the blue sky. It was amazing what he could find - the internet truly represented freedom in terms of virtually unlimited access to information.

The computer room was supervised by Steve Diggle, an overweight and bored guard, selected not for his IT skills, but because he had bad feet and wasn't suited to other more rigorous duties. Steve would look over Don's shoulder from time to time, asking in a disinterested voice what he was doing. Don usually had his Fantasy Football League page open and would pop it up on screen whenever Steve approached, leading to a brief exchange about the merits and demerits of certain footballers. Millionaires, most of them, and Don planned to join them.

Don was busy planning his escape. He'd worked out how to embezzle money from bank accounts online and had researched suitable countries to go to. He'd settled on Venezuela for three reasons: there was no extradition treaty with the UK; it was easy to set up a bank account over the internet; and residency status was given if a property was purchased for over US$250,000.

"A sunny place for shady people," he said absent-mindedly.

"What's that?" Steve asked, not even bothering to look up from his copy of The Sun.

"Oh, err... just looking at your headline and thinking about all those villains living in Spain."

The well-fed prison guard grunted and glanced at the front-page headline, 'Costa Criminal Arrested'. It was July 2015, and the nation was enjoying in a few days of warm, sunny weather. "Don't worry about them, most of 'em will be back 'ere soon."

Don had taken an online course in Adobe Photoshop and had now created a forged letter, on official headed paper, granting his early release from prison. It bore the name and signature of the High Court judge who'd presided over his case. He'd scanned the judge's signature from a copy of his case ruling that his solicitor had sent him.

He asked Steve's permission to print something, distracting him just at the time the printer was spewing it out, and put it in the pre-prepared envelope bearing the address of his solicitor. He would slip it to his brother Jimmy on his next visit so he could put a stamp on and post it from the nearest post office to the High Court.

If this worked, he could forget about tunnelling out or going over the wall and wading through the marshes of the Thames Estuary, like a modern-day Magwitch from his favourite book, *Great Expectations* by Charles Dickens. Magwitch had escaped from a prison hulk, a huge, floating prison ship moored along the Thames Estuary in Victorian times.

Don was no brooding hulk of a man like Magwitch; he was short and tubby, an exercise-avoider with poor eyesight. It wasn't for him, sloshing waist-deep through mud and effluent. He was a white-collar criminal, and would walk out through the front gate, smiling at the grim-faced guards and maybe even daring to shake their hands.

As for his crime, he'd embezzled fifty thousand pounds from his employer, a well-known high street bank. This had been the last resort of a desperate assistant branch manager, as his daughter, Lily, was dying of a rare form of bone cancer, and he and his now ex-wife had wanted to give her once last shot at survival by raising the funds for an experimental course of treatment in the USA. He'd set up an online fundraising appeal page, and funnelled his embezzled funds to it in dribs and drabs. The treatment didn't work and Lily passed away, having fallen into a coma, her suffering ended, in a private US clinic. Don felt no remorse for his actions, recalling with bitterness the helpless shrug of their daughter's health care consultant. Surely any parent would do everything they could for their child?

His employment prospects were now ruined by his criminal record and his family was no more. He just wanted out, and the prospect of a life on the run held a curious thrill. Now he'd applied his analytical mind to the means of escape.

Three weeks later, he received a phone call from his solicitor with the unexpected and remarkable news that his release date had been brought forward by four years and he'd be released the following Monday.

"Ahh, the sweet smell of freedom!" Don made a show of sniffing the air as he stepped out of the front gate, eyed disdainfully by the screws, and walked across the road to where his brother was waiting. They stopped off for a pint and to catch up on family gossip at a country pub on their way to Jimmy's home in Portsmouth.

Don knew it would probably take just a few days before the "mistake" was discovered, so he wasted no time in making his travel arrangements. He'd applied for an Irish passport whilst in prison, forging a birth certificate for his late grandfather and claiming Irish citizenship. This was a standard British birth certificate, but from the province of Ulster. Anyone born in Northern Ireland, their children, and grandchildren, were eligible to apply for Irish citizenship.

He'd even altered his own name and his grandfather's name to distance himself as much as possible from his real British identity. Ahh, the good old Irish - less interested in detail and more in widening the pool of the Irish diaspora. Don was now Dennis O'Dwyer.

He cleared out his bank account, told Jimmy he was taking a trip to France, and boarded a ferry. It was best that his brother knew nothing of his plans as the police would soon be all over him like a rash. This would be the last time he'd use his British passport. In France, he made his way to Paris and set about opening a bank account under his new identity. Then he bought a return airline ticket to Caracas, costing €2,000. He got a tourist visa and bought some clothes that were more suitable for a tropical climate.

Posing as a tourist, he cleared customs in Caracas with no issues, and walked out to the hot and dusty taxi rank. A bored-looking taxi driver took him on the scenic route, passing beautiful beaches with swaying palms, golden sands, and few people, then around the streets and pretty squares of Caracas, on the way to his hotel. He was struck by the elegant decay of the once-majestic old colonial buildings, reflecting the sun's glare from their paint-chipped, dirty white walls.

His high-ceilinged room had a balcony overlooking a pretty square. In the centre was a small park with a dozen araguaney trees, resplendent with bright yellow blooms. He smelled the fragrant air and smiled. He ate alone that evening in the shabby restaurant and retired to bed early.

The following morning, Dennis O'Dwyer, Irish national abroad, made the short walk to the Banco Centrale de Venezuela. He showed his passport to the bank clerk and asked if he could check his bank balance. This was done - a cool one and a half million dollars. He withdrew some cash and went looking for an estate agent. His plan was to buy an apartment in the city centre for a little over a quarter of a million, then apply for residency status. He would also enrol for Spanish classes and get into the customs and culture of his new home as quickly as possible.

All was well, until the following day when he received a phone call at the hotel from his bank. Had he authorised a withdrawal of funds from his account? He hadn't, and said he'd be over there right away. To his horror, he discovered that his bank account had been cleaned out and the balance was now nil. He'd been the victim of a fraudster! He raged at the impassive manager, who looked down on him with a slightly mocking expression, as if he could see into his corrupt soul. Perhaps he was the thief?

As he left the building, shielding his eyes from the bright sunlight, he reflected on the unpredictable and lawless world of a criminal - who do you complain to if you're a thief who has been robbed? He dabbed the sweat from his eyes with a large, white hankie. No point in dwelling on it. The taxi driver who drove him from the airport appeared in front of him. Dennis asked to be taken to the nearest internet cafe. What goes around comes around... he would set about relieving some other unsuspecting account holders of their funds.

"A sunny place for shady people, indeed," he mused, as the battered taxi edged its way past noisy pedestrians and a donkey cart full of bananas, the driver shouting out the window to add to the cacophony. Out of the corner of his eye, he saw movement in the opposite footwell.

"Aaaagh!" he screamed, causing the taxi driver to jam on the brakes and the battered old taxi to skid to a halt beside the road in a cloud of dust.

"What is it, señor!? Have you been shot?" the driver said, spinning his droopy moustached face around in alarm.

"Shot? No, of course not. It's a spider!" Dennis pointed to a large, black hairy spider crawling on the floor, no doubt just looking for a way out.

"Oh signor! That's just a friendly tarantula! There are many, because of the bananas, but most don't bite." He jumped out and opened the rear passenger door, bending down and skilfully scooping up the offending spider in his hands and throwing it into the bushes. The driver got back behind the wheel and rejoined the road without signalling or looking, straight into the path of a wobbling, overcrowded minibus. Amidst much hooting and cursing, he sped off along the pot-holed road.

"Have you lost many customers to gun shots?" Dennis asked the driver, once there was a clear stretch of road ahead.

"Only once, señor, in all my years of driving this taxi. Here we are, señor, the internet cafe."

Dennis surveyed the peeling cream paint on the pock-marked building's façade with disdain. Were those bullet holes? One gunshot victim was one too many. He pulled out a 100 Bolivar note from his pocket and handed it to the grinning driver. Their currency, he mused, is named after a famous revolutionary who took from the rich to give to the poor – a South American Robin Hood. Would Simon Bolivar have approved of his defrauding a bank? He smiled at the thought as he got out of the taxi, happy to have his feet back on terra firma after a hair-raising ride. He arched his back and stretched, feeling more Butch Cassidy than the Sundance Kid. He was the brains, not the brawn.

"It may be a challenge, but I'll be a rich man yet in this backward, but beguiling banana republic," he muttered as he mopped his brow.

Valentine's Day

Val Hanwell, basking in the warm glow of having recently been promoted to marketing services manager, was briefing his new team; two quite different but equally eager to please executives. The age difference between Val and keen, young executive, Sally, may have only been five years, but in terms of experience at the corporate coalface, Val was light years ahead of her. As for Dan, he was the latest AI bot with enhanced human features, 2050 model, fresh from a factory in Japan.

They worked in the marketing division of the Port and Docks company that reported directly to a board minister. Companies represented sectors of the economy under the Britannia Freeport Corporation that had seized control of an ailing Britain a dozen years earlier, ending parliamentary democracy and breaking up the union, then going it alone as a rump England, soon rebranded as Britannia.

The Statute Book had been reduced to little more than a pro-regime pamphlet as most laws had been repealed and the Supreme Court was a toothless stooge that doled out pro-corporation rulings. Personal freedoms and rights were deemed unnecessary as the ruling elite considered themselves best placed to make decisions on behalf of the citizens. But the waves were now ruling Britannia, and the Corporation's current focus was on relocating settlements to higher ground as the island shrank before a greedy, relentless sea.

"Right, we've got to produce a minister's report from the latest market research findings of our survey on attitudes to corporation policy. Upload the data. The clock's ticking. We need to turn this around in a week. Dan, you list the main findings and I'll come in on the recommendations. Sally, pick out the positive pro-corporation points for the PR campaign and make a separate folder for negatives. I've just sent you both the upload code for the data. The PR flunkies are empty vessels waiting to be filled and we'll pour some soothing pro-corporation sentiments onto their sweat-stained tablets."

He paused for effect. Sally blinked her long lashes twice, then put her head down over her tablet, tapping furiously at her keyboard. Dan elicited a mimicked cough and his right eye flashed green, signalling comprehension and compliance.

Val turned to look out of the window at the wide lagoon that was once the River Thames Estuary. Sunlight glinting off glass tower points protruding from the crinkly blanket of white-capped green held a strange, poetic fascination. A floating hologram advertising sandy beach holidays to the regime-friendly Cape Verde Islands, added to the surreal, soothing effect. Was the lagoon rippling more than usual?

He spun his chair round to face them and met Sally's smile as she looked up from her tablet. Dan wore his standard complaint expression.

"Uploaded the files? Great. Familiarise yourselves with the data, noting the key points. We'll go over them at tomorrow's meeting and firm up our strategy. Any questions?"

Sally held up her hand, ever the eager student. "Sir, with the final evacuation notice having gone into red, we've only got three weeks until relocation to our new quarters in Britannia New Town in the Peak District. How shall we prioritise our time?"

Val paused whilst framing his reply. "I take it you've both been given collection dates and times for evacuation from your apartments?"

She nodded and Dan droned, "Yes, Mr Hanwell," then, "I am sensing a tremor in the building."

Sure enough, there was a slight vibration, and both Val and Sally noticed ripples on the surface of Val's coffee.

"Mr Hanwell!" Sally yelped, "it's not safe in this building. Only last week my friend was injured when her building collapsed! Should we evacuate?" Her wide eyes pleaded with him for salvation.

Val held his desk with both hands, as if he was on a ship pitching in heavy seas. "Erm, no. At least not until the siren sounds. Just compose yourself, Sally, keep calm and carry on. As the directive in the evacuation manual advises."

Her lower lip was trembling, and her eyes welled up with tears.

Val addressed his AI executive. "Dan, can you tell if it's an earth tremor or the building is, erm, in a distressed state?" Val was aware that the frequency of buildings collapsing had increased as the corrosive effects of salt water and tidal movements had eaten into brick and concrete. The London skyline, once resolute in its conceit, was gradually disappearing beneath the pernicious tidal lagoon, the jagged teeth of an ancient gradually being pulled to leave submerged grey gums that mocked the corporation's bullish narrative of a buoyant Britannia, proud and defiant.

"Buildings were designed to be above water level, not in it," Val muttered.

Dan's blank gaze did little to ease his jitters. "I detect a consistent vibration pattern and therefore conclude that it is the effects of an earth tremor. If the building was subsiding, I would be able to calculate the angle of its leaning, sir. It is not leaning."

"Good. Then a slight earth tremor it is. Back to your desks and get started on analysing the data. Sally, if the building moves, the siren will go off and we'll have plenty of time to get out. Off you go."

Earth tremors weren't a new thing. "We get it. The planet is angry," Val muttered as he spun around and watched the hypnotic symmetry of the ripples across the wide Thames lagoon gradually diminish, like Mother Nature smoothing the wrinkles on her apron.

After a minute of idle reflection, Val looked up, sensing a change in the office atmosphere. The chatter had died away, like birds experiencing an eclipse. An eerie hush descended before Val heard a familiar humming noise. The hover-mobile of their new marketing director glided across the open-plan space, heading for her office at the far end of the room. Alisha Bosun-Smythe, ASB to the staff, didn't look left or right, nor smile or acknowledge anyone in her new division as she glided into her glass booth and plugged into her port. Her appointment had sent shockwaves through their cosy, friendly section of twelve easy-going and sociable individuals, jerking them out of their complacency. Two new AI bots had added to their disquiet. Everyone was aware that the impending relocation was also an opportunity for a reduction in staff. Streamlining, they called it.

The unemployed were increasingly being recruited for compulsory overseas postings in exchange for trade deals that had led to the subversive social media hash tag, "profitoverpeople". Population reduction measures were an ongoing priority of a desperate corporation. Few ever returned from their overseas postings.

ASB came with the reputation of a corporate troubleshooter. Her online profile boasted that she was an accomplished downsizer, saving divisions thousands off their budgets. Despite his recent promotion, Alisha already had Val in her sights. She had issued him a warning memo on trumped-up charges, with a vague exhortation to "do better" and to "buck up your ideas", or else. A lawyer friend had only increased Val's disquiet by advising him to collect evidence of work achievements as this looked like the opening salvo in an attempt to remove him for incompetence. He had his suspicions that she might be an AI bot, programmed to have a mean streak.

"Me, incompetent?" he seethed, reliving the moment, then sought to dispel the unhappy thought from his head. He swivelled away from his desk and sought calm in the landscape of chugging dredgers and a naval frigate negotiating the grey stumps that were once the Thames Barrier, only visible now at low tide. In the distance bobbed an old ocean liner now repurposed as a prison for political dissidents. From his impressive vantage point on the eighth floor of the London Port and Docks House, standing in a row of forlorn buildings that once lined the south bank, he could follow the slow progress of a barge carrying dredged-up mud and assorted human waste slowly downriver into an ever-widening lagoon, until finally merging with the grey smog cloud that hung permanently overhead. He wondered how many millions of people had lived and worked on the banks of the ever-busy River Thames before the great flood had wiped out a property market that was once worth billions.

Val's sprits were instantly lifted when a familiar face flashed up on screen. "Hi Tabitha, how's it going? Are we still on for this evening?"

Tabitha and Val had been on the same marketing degree course, and now both worked for companies in the high-rise city of canals. They'd become close friends, meeting to play virtual racquetball, socialise and compare their experiences of corporate life and office politics. He felt a strong desire for his beautiful friend, despite her shallow nature and fawning, pro-regime sympathies. Sometimes it was a struggle to maintain the pretence that he didn't fancy her and be nonchalant in her company... whilst talking about invented girlfriends.

"Sure", she said in a voice that suggested she was preoccupied. He could see the top of her blonde head as she rooted around in her desk drawer on his curved 3D screen. She looked great in 3D. "Erm... 8 pm at yours, right? I'll collect you from your landing stage and we'll hover over to the sports centre. Did you make the booking?"

Val absently squeezed a rubber stress-ball. "Yes, all booked for twenty-thirty, so don't be late."

They both commuted by boats from their respective satellite suburban islands. They made the most of the work-hard-play-hard lifestyle of bright young things in a city of boats, floating bars, and restaurants. In a recent move by the corporation, the city centre was now a restricted zone for workers with the correct authorisation.

Val had other friends for cultural activities like going to gigs and shows, but Tabitha was his regular racquetball partner and they tried to meet up once a month for an hour of intense, lung-bursting sport, followed by a meal and drinks. He really looked forward to this special time with the iconic, untouchable Tabitha, but after each meeting, he was left with a hollow feeling and a yearning for a perfect partner.

Val had recently disentangled himself from a university relationship that had staggered on for years until finally dying from lack of interest and commitment on both parts. The "I love you's" had developed a hollow ring as they had slowly drifted apart. Now he and Hilary had been downgraded to "social media friends".

He was happy to be taking a breather and have some time out from dating to fall back on the company of his friends; although as his name day – Valentine's Day – approached, he was starting to feel agitated by the lack of a date for the Corporate Achievers' Ball. These were a series of tiered events, so he'd now have to leave his former executive friends and their wild party to attend the middle manager's ball on the next tier up.

Tabitha, on the other hand, was in a long-term relationship with a very vain and good-looking guy called Bart who worked for a music company. Val could see the appeal - superficially, they looked like the perfect couple, all blonde hair, blue eyes, and wide, toothsome smiles. They must have looked great together at music industry events, mixing with pop stars, celebrities, and execs. She rarely spoke about him, and they didn't seem to spend much time together - the occasional weekend away and record company events mainly. Val had only met him once as she was careful to keep the various strands of her social life separate.

Val logged off just before five, cleared his desk and made his way out into the open-plan space where the executives and support staff had their desks - bordered on one side by shelving units standing six-feet high that had once housed bound volumes of market research data, but now had neat rows of hard drives in project folders interspersed with potted plants.

"Valentine! Come to me!" ASB's shrill voice stopped everyone in their tracks, and all eyes fell on Val. He ambled apprehensively across the grey patterned carpet like a man going to the gallows.

She waved him into her glass cubicle and asked how it was going in a manner that suggested she didn't really care. He shuffled awkwardly, not having been invited to sit and, choosing his words carefully, gave an upbeat report on the arrival of the new data set from the corporation survey and his delegation of tasks to the executives. *Be an indispensable cog in the machine, Val.* ASB wasn't interested in what they actually did, more in how the relationships were between the staff, always looking for any signs of discord that she could exploit.

"Are you making use of the new robot-thing?"

"Erm, yes, I've given Dan, the V16 AI bot, a data compilation task, and I've briefed Sally to take a more nuanced analytical approach to the data. I'll bring both strands together for a report and board presentation."

She looked up with cold, grey eyes and blinked once before speaking. "Good. If you mess this one up, Hanwell, like your last job, then your brief career as a manager will come to a shuddering end. I do believe you've been promoted above your competence." Her eyes narrowed and her voice dropped to a low, menacing growl.

"I wasn't responsible for the mess up..." his voice tailed away as she pushed off from her desk, the loose skin of her jowls wobbling like a turkey resisting Christmas round-up and, with a curt, "follow me", she hovered out into the office as terminals were being shut down and staff were getting ready to go home. *Did she even have legs?* Val thought, miserably, as he followed behind her hovering metal vessel. Shocking injuries and amputations of the many survivors who'd been trapped under collapsed buildings had become a common feature of London life. She couldn't leave without publicly humiliating at least one of them, and this time, it was the turn of one of the marketing executives - a nervous and sweaty young man called Ian, whom Val had recruited personally after a visit to his old university two years earlier.

"This is one of the worst executive summaries I've ever read!" she thundered, spinning a disk that clattered onto his desk. "It reads like a schoolboy's essay culled from first generation AI machine code. It lacks analytical insight. You need to up your game young man..." and so it went on.

Val exchanged glances with the others but kept a straight face. No time for levity. *Not much I can do for him*, he thought glumly, *she's lining up one in three for the chop and the bets are off on poor Ian now. I wonder what the office odds are on me surviving the cull?*

Val made his way in gloomy silence to the men's locker room and put on his anti-smog suit. He was adjusting his oxygen feed as he walked out, when he literally bumped into a young woman.

"Oh, really sorry, here - let me get that for you," he said, bending to pick up a fallen bag. As he stood, he found himself face to face with a work colleague he hardly knew - Nisha Myers, a senior research executive.

"Oh, no problem, Mr Hanwell, I can see you're in a rush to leave."

"Please, Nisha, call me Val. I... must dash for my commute boat, bye."

She put her hand on his arm to halt him and blurted out, "I need to speak to you about something. As you know, my manager, Mr Zelinski, is off work..."

"Strictly speaking, you're not in my section, but in view of his absence, come and see me in the morning," he replied, edging away. His recent promotion had only just made him senior to her. *Hmmm, attractive, pleasant, and with a lovely smile... why haven't I noticed her before?*

Val stepped out through the glass lobby doors onto the floating platform in a humid and hazy late afternoon, picking his way to the queue at pick-up point nine. Outside the air-conditioned building, he instinctively took a draw on his oxygen mouthpiece. The advice was to take a puff every ten minutes, to increase the amount of oxygen reaching the lungs when outside. He could now travel in the more spacious and comfortable front compartment of the commuter boat, as his promotion had moved him up from worker classification C to B. He couldn't wait to tell Tabitha. She was already a B.

Once seated, the thirty-foot launch edged into the left lane and moved south, keeping between the floating, fluorescent buoys that demarked the channel of what was once Blackfriars Road. At Elephant and Castle, the boat navigated a semi-circular course around the reinstated statue of an elephant with a castle on its back, on a thirty-foot steel pole that marked the centrepiece of a watery roundabout.

Val's apartment was on the Crystal Palace Island, one of a dozen islands that dotted the vast South London lake. The boat would travel on to the Surrey Hills and towns such as Redhill, where many London-based workers lived. As he alighted, he noted a 30-seater drone landing at the adjacent landing pad, a more expensive mode of travel, often the reserve of directors and highly paid utility maintenance workers.

*****

That evening, Val spent a good half hour on his appearance in his self-cleaning bathroom. Having showered off the city grime, he applied some scented moisturiser to his face and a slick of gel to his hair. He was of average height and slim build, with collar-length, straight brown hair, cut to the regulation corporate length in a style that never dated.

He buzzed Tabitha in when her voice crackled on the intercom. She was disarmingly turned out in a turquoise leisure suit as she stood smiling in his doorway, her racquet bag slung over one shoulder. He kissed her lightly on the cheek, inhaling her familiar sweet scent, and said, "We'd better get going."

He grabbed his bag and followed her to the elevator, admiring her cute wiggle and the swish of her blonde ponytail. He didn't know whether he should keep complimenting her on her appearance - she always looked incredible no matter what she wore. *Act as if she were just another friend, no one special*, for this was their relationship. Whenever he was in her company, other men would stare, which irked him more than her; she'd long perfected the art of appearing not to notice.

Val felt like he was out of his league with her, not just because she was so good-looking, but because she came from a top corporate family and had been the best student on their course, getting A-stars in virtually every subject and passing with a distinction. He'd found it hard work and had to toil late into the night, cramming information into his head and worrying about his project coursework. His was just a pass, but good enough when combined with his degree and couple of years' relevant work experience to get the job he wanted. *Thursday's child has far to go.*

It was a warm, summer's evening and they chatted about work as they exited the hover taxi and entered the leisure centre. They swiped in and went to their respective changing rooms to leave their things in the lockers. On court, they put on their goggles and started to warm up, knocking the small cyber-ball against the virtual wall with increasing power. Val slyly checked her out by hitting the ball into the front corners of the court so that she had to lunge forward to return it, lifting his goggles momentarily to get a better view of her perfect, apple-shaped bum contained in a pair of black figure-hugging Lycra shorts.

Her baggy white T-shirt would sometimes fly up, giving him a glimpse of her svelte figure and sporty black crop top enclosing her perfect, round breasts. *Concentrate on the game,* he self-admonished.

When they'd just started their duels, he'd been the better player, but Tabitha had improved in skill and fitness and their matches were now keenly contested. Only occasionally would he succeed in his primary objective – to run her around to the extent that she'd get so hot that she'd have to take off her T-shirt.

After the game, they stood by the oxygenating machine, taking alternate mouthfuls of clean air; then separated to shower and change before making their way into the Crystal Palace mall. A branch of Moonbeams had recently opened, and they went there for the vintage American diner experience.

Val wanted to ask her about her boyfriend, and how it was going with him, secretly hoping it was going badly, but he refrained, knowing the topic was out of bounds. Most of their conversations were work-related and they used each other to let off steam from their stressful, deadline-dominated lives. He told her about Ian's public humiliation by ASB, and the increasing pressure on him due to his co-manager being off sick. She half-listened and came back with a similar story of corporate bullying - but not directly affecting her, of course.

Val's career progression had evolved more organically; he'd waited patiently for his opportunity for promotion to come, whereas Tabitha had already been promoted twice and her route to a seat on the board of directors was all planned out. Her parents were senior party members and she had, inevitably, made it to B-class before him. She smiled when he proudly told her that he could now ride in the same compartment as her.

He genuinely enjoyed her company; she laughed at his jokes and was quick-witted in reply. They ate, drank, and giggled - this was the high-point of his month, and after the meal, he escorted her to her hover taxi, said goodnight, and pecked her on the cheek.

He hummed "You're Beautiful", one of his favourite oldies, as he rode the elevator to his floor, but his musing was tinged with sadness - she was a goddess and he a mere mortal, staring longingly up at the clouds surrounding her Mount Olympus.

Tabitha had casually mentioned that she was going to the music industry's celebrity-studded category-B Valentine's Day ball with her boyfriend Bart. Val admitted he was still searching for a suitable date, using his recent promotion to B class as an excuse.

"Oh yes, you must find a B, darling," Tabitha had said, "if you want to sit on our table." He had taken this casual, throwaway remark as a taunt, or a challenge, that did little to soothe his agitation.

*****

The following morning, Val checked on the work in progress with Dan and Sally, then took the lift to the reception area where a visitor was waiting to see him.

"Hi, I'm Valentine Hanwell, marketing services manager, pleased to meet you." Val shook the hand of a taller, well-built Norwegian man, casually dressed in a roll neck jumper and zip-up waterproof jacket. Val wore his work suit of matching blue trousers and collarless jacket with the Port and Docks company logo of a ship's 3D bow jutting out from his left breast.

"Magnus Olafsson, tidal manager at NorFlow company," came the reply. Val winced as his hand was crushed in a firm handshake. First point to Norway.

Val guided his visitor to the meeting room that he'd booked. Visitors weren't allowed on the upper floors, following a rash of terrorist attacks.

"Take a seat, Mr Olafsson, may I call you Magnus?"

"Please do, thank you." The big man wedged his behind into a small bucket seat and placed a tablet on the table.

"How was your journey?" Val asked.

Magnus grinned. "We flew over a North Sea littered with icebergs moving south, now empty of rigs and ships. It's become too dangerous to navigate."

Such visuals weren't shown on Britannia news as the extent of disruptions to sea trade was carefully managed information. The effects of the closure of the east coast container ports on the struggling economy was kept quiet. Of the corporation's five flagship freeports, only Southampton and Avonmouth were still functioning.

Val smiled and moved swiftly on to his prepared speech. "Thank you for coming to brief us on Norway's experiences of dealing with relocation away from the coastal areas. I'm sure there's much we can learn from each other. I've been cleared by our board of directors to show you the new video of our plans and projections. As your host, I'll go first." Val tapped his tablet and a large, flat screen lit up on the wall. He tapped again and the lights dimmed, then excused himself to fetch some coffees from the canteen whilst his visitor watched the half-hour presentation.

Val sipped his coffee until the presentation had ended, then raised the lights. "Well? What are your first impressions?"

His visitor beamed through a neatly trimmed beard and shifted in his seat to try and find some comfort before speaking. "Nice drone camera shots. But the description of your ongoing evacuation lacks detail. For example, how many were living in the Thames flood plain when the first tidal surge breached the Thames Barrier? How many were successfully relocated and how many lives were lost? Also, I'd like to know more on the engineering solutions to contain the tidal peaks whilst the relocation was taking place. This is merely a PR video, Mr Hanwell."

Val blushed and tapped a note on his tablet. "Well, shall we watch your video presentation first, and then answer each other's questions?"

"But Valentine, mine is a detailed analysis of tidal flow and a stepped relocation plan over a number of years, produced by engineers and scientists, with plenty of tables of data as appendices. Furthermore, and I'm referring to the rumours of your losses, we lost no one to drowning events. They're not the same thing."

A detailed plan was precisely what Val had hoped for, and what he'd been briefed to collect, whilst disclosing as little as possible of their own feeble response to a natural catastrophe whose consequences were lied about and covered up by the Britannia Corporation.

"We had minimal deaths during the early stages of evacuation, contrary to the false social media reports. I've got some tables of data to give you, Magnus. Let's proceed with your presentation, then we can discuss the details and exchange data." A vexing memory of the rows of body bags on the dock wall at low tide suddenly floated into his mind.

Magnus nodded and twinned his tablet with the wall screen. The two men sat back and watched. Val smiled in the darkened room at the detail and animated models showing ingenious methods of moving entire buildings onto floating pontoons, something that had been tried in London a few years ago with disastrous results.

When the presentation was over, Val answered Magnus's questions in a vague way, adding that the detail was in the data sets that he'd exchange with him. Magnus answered Val's questions with references to technical aspects that went over Val's head.

"I'm not convinced that we'll learn much from your experiences, Mr Hanwell, except maybe how not to do it!" Magnus said, followed by a deep, rumbling laugh.

"There's plenty of detail of ten years of innovation in our full report, I can assure you, Magnus, and Britannia engineering remains a world leader," Val oozed, feeling decidedly uncomfortable at his reluctant role in spinning a line for the corporation. But he and Magnus were being listened to, and Val felt he had no choice but to act out his part. It seemed to him that much of their marketing output was merely papering over the cracks or helping to shore up the falsehoods. He felt a tad foolish before the derisory smirk of his confident visitor.

"Well, I must fulfil our promise, so now I'll transfer my files to you. Please give me the codes," Magnus said. Codes were exchanged, they uploaded each other's files, rose, and shook hands.

Val followed Magnus outside, sniffing at the cooling air. "Will you be staying overnight? I can recommend a good restaurant that's just opened."

Magnus signalled to an attendant to ready his drone, then turned to Val. "Moonbeams? When you've been to one, you've been to them all. No thanks." He paused and studied the slim Briton. "You know, Valentine, you people are so submissive. You work in collapsing buildings, too scared to complain. No, I'm not staying any longer than is necessary. Goodbye, and good luck."

The two men shook hands again and Val was left with his own thoughts as he watched the Norwegian's heli-drone lift up into the darkening sky. The draft blew Val's hair into a wild, uncombed mess. Normally, he would immediately comb it back into shape, but instead, he turned to walk towards the riverside edge of the platform. He gazed over the lagoon of drowned structures and the river lane running through it, demarked by yellow buoys, as a bank of fog wrapped its grey tentacles around the tops of the twin towers of the submerged Tower Bridge. The metal spar between the towers and the drawbridge flaps had long since been removed, and now the tower tops were surrounded by orange floats that rose and fell with the tide, warning off the rivercraft.

"Monuments to a drowned world," he muttered, turning away.

Val returned to his desk, relieved that his meeting had gone to plan. He then typed out a brief memo and sent the data files to the technical team, his boss, and her board director. ASB wasn't in the office, so Val could relax and turn his attention to what he would be doing that evening, the eve of Saint Valentine's Day.

He'd already found a suitable date by selecting an appropriate manager-level dating agency. After all, he had a pair of tickets to the middle manager's prestigious Valentine's Day ball and needed a partner.

He had spent a couple of days evaluating the various leading online dating agencies before settling on one. He'd completed the profile questionnaire, paid a three-month fee, and recorded a fifteen-second profile video. Based on his answers, he was sent half a dozen potential matches, and he carefully studied their video presentations, noting their appearance, status, and location.

Val had made his choice, a woman named Anne who held a similar position in another corporation, close to his own age. She lived and worked in another part of the city and her profile and photo gave the impression of a fun, organised, independent-minded, and attractive individual. After an initial email exchange, followed by a video link conversation, they agreed to meet for dinner. That date was this evening, and Val was pleased that his boss wasn't around to delay his departure. If it went well, he would invite Anne to be his date for the following evening's Valentine's Day ball.

He was fascinated by the dating profile that had been created for him and clicked on the virtual dating adviser link. A woman's smiling face filled his screen. He leaned back and listened to her synthetic voice.

Your responses to the dating appeal questions revealed that you're an introvert rather than an extrovert, meaning you're thoughtful and may hide your feelings. You're also a judger rather than a perceiver, meaning you're organised and like closure. And finally, you're a sensor rather than an intuitor, meaning you're practical and have an eye for detail.

Val hit pause, leaned back in his chair, and thought about this, deciding that it was a true reflection of his personality. He *was* introvert, organised, and practical. He hated any kind of mess or an incomplete task. Magnus's parting shot had irked him. Was he little more than a compliant functionary in a cold, uncaring corporation, challenged to keep using his initiative to stay one step ahead of being replaced by an AI bot? He clicked off pause and resumed the briefing.

Now Val, here are some tips to remember when dating: bear in mind that you can sometimes forget to say what you're thinking, including that you're having a good time. Share your thoughts with your date. You love to understand things, including people. Sometimes that can make your conversations seem a bit more of an interrogation than you intend. Back off a little and listen to your date. You can easily get diverted from the present and disappear inside your own head. Do your best to stay in the moment with your date, or you may appear bored or disinterested.

"Okay, I can see myself in most of this," Val muttered, hurriedly shutting down and returning to the present, as Nisha knocked politely and came in. Her desk was on the far side of the office, and she reported to Miles Zelinski, the other market research manager, who'd been absent for several weeks with a stress-related condition that had manifested itself in a nasty attack of shingles. Val knew little about her, except that she was a quiet and conscientious number-cruncher. She swiped her hand under her skirt as she sat, crossing her shapely, brown legs. Val looked up from her knee and was suddenly drawn into her large, deep brown eyes.

"Hi, Nisha, my apologies again for bumping into you yesterday, what can I do for you?"

"Oh, that's alright," she sweetly replied, "it's just… I spotted an anomaly in the data, and in the absence of my manager, I wanted to bring it to someone's attention."

"An anomaly, eh? We don't have those very often. Show me."

Sure enough, there was a problem with the data set. She'd calculated that some of the totals on the cross-tabulated fields didn't correspond to the totals at the foot of the columns.

"Yes, you're right. These are errors. I'll get onto the research company. Well done, you!" Val grinned at the thought that this might push him up in ASB's estimation.

She smiled like a pupil who'd been given a gold star and he noted her full lips and button nose in the centre of her pretty face.

"Let's keep this between ourselves until I get some feedback from our agency." Val nodded his head slightly in the direction of his boss's office. If ASB caught wind of any problems, it would spell trouble, certainly for Miles, but possibly for himself as well. His instinct was to cover for his stricken colleague and only present it to her as a minor problem that had been identified and dealt with efficiently.

He admired her shapely figure as she walked out of his cubbyhole and glided across the open-plan office. He sighed and shook his head. The approaching Valentine's Day ball and his impending date seemed to have aroused his manly instincts. He felt like a strutting stag surveying the herd. It must be the time of year, he mused, as he tidied up his desk.

On his way home, Val reflected that his profile as an analytical, introverted, fact-obsessed person made him well-suited to his career in market research. He would channel his skills in preparation for his date to avoid coming across as disinterested and bored. Take an interest in your date; get her to talk about herself; be sure to listen; have follow-up questions; and try to establish some common ground. More importantly, remember everything she tells you.

At home, Val went through his grooming process and then met Anne, his date, at the restaurant they'd agreed on. His first impressions were good, and they chatted amicably over dinner. Common interests were established, and a good rapport flowed. Val was pleasantly surprised by her neat and tidy appearance. She was a bit taller and broader than the usually-petite women he tended to go for, but he was prepared to overlook that. She had crystal-clear blue eyes and a nervous, slightly manic laugh, but on the whole, he liked her manner and how she looked.

He invited Anne to his flat for a nightcap, and she agreed. They sat on his sofa, listening to music, whilst he sipped red wine. Anne didn't drink alcohol and was curiously abstemious of all offers of a drink. The attempted cuddle and kiss were awkward at first, then more relaxed. She said she was shy and asked him to dim the lights. He approved of her as a match and had made up his mind to invite her to tomorrow's ball. If that went well, then maybe a new relationship would blossom.

Anne excused herself, and when she returned, she seemed agitated and fired a series of lifestyle questions at Val, a list, almost, including asking why he'd put his hand on her thigh.

This put Val on the defensive. He was getting slightly irritated with the odd interrogation, and this soon led to a full-on row. She was angry at his deflection of her questions and kept repeating them, as none of his responses proved satisfactory.

"That's just how it is between men and women!" Val yelled in exasperation. He was taken aback by the sudden switch in her manner from calm and collected to being aggressive and confrontational, as if the wrong button had been pressed.

"You've no right to talk to me like that!" she stormed, "you're just like my ex, he constantly criticised me and put me down!" She started pacing the room, scratching her head, and making unusual jerking motions, ranting in an increasingly loud voice about how her ex had treated her badly and eventually left her for one of her friends. *Crikey, she's got issues.* Val found it odd that she kept repeating the same phrases over and over. Fuelled by the red wine, he tried to make light of the situation with a flippant remark. Unfortunately, it had the opposite effect as, with a wild look in her eyes, Anne rushed at him and started pummelling her fists against his chest and trying to scratch his face.

Val grabbed her wrists to protect his face. She was surprisingly strong, and Val struggled to push her away. He ran out of the living room and locked himself in the bathroom for safety. Taking out his phone, he quickly scrolled through his contacts list, not sure who to call. He passed the 'S's and stopped at Tabitha. She lived nearby, was a feisty character, and maybe it would take a woman to calm Anne down. By now, Anne was banging on the bathroom door, demanding that he come out and stop hiding from her, but she was still in a rage and he had no intention of coming out. He called

Tabitha, told her what had happened, and held the phone up towards the door so she could hear the banging and shouting. The fuzzy picture showed her in bra straps in her bedroom.

"Alright, I'll be over in thirty minutes, just stay in there until I come to your door. I'll get one of your neighbours to buzz me in. I'll wear my sports gear and make out that we were supposed to meet for racquetball, okay?"

"Yeah, please hurry," he wailed. His attempts to pacify Anne had amounted to nothing. It seemed as if she'd really gone off the deep end and was totally out of control, crying and banging the door with her fists and her head.

Whilst sitting on the toilet, his head in his hands, waiting to be rescued, Val had a vision of himself as a tiny, cowering figure surrounded by tall, angry, and aggressive women, crowding in on him and suffocating him. He'd become a pathetic pawn in a gender power game.

There was his boss, schoolyard bully ASB, the beautiful and brainy Tabitha, and now the psychotic Anne. Even his talented young executive, Sally, would soon be pushing at his door. *What's going on?* He felt intimidated by all of them.

It seemed like an eternity, but eventually there was a buzz at the front door. There was a momentary silence from Anne, then he could hear Tabitha's voice.

"Is everything alright in there? Can I speak to Val?" Anne had let her in - presumably to make out everything was fine.

"Val is in the bathroom," she said in an even, unemotional voice.

Val felt that it was safe to come out, although no sooner was he in the living room than Anne rushed towards him, screaming with rage. Tabitha reacted quickly and put herself between the two of them. She grabbed Anne by her arms, and soon they were pulling each other's hair. Amid shrieks and screams, they were then grappling on the carpet, exchanging slaps, and clawing at each other's faces.

Val was both shocked and fascinated. Tabitha seemed to be winning the brawl. She looked as sexy as ever in her figure-hugging shorts and tight T-shirt, and she soon gained the upper hand, pinning the shocked Anne to the carpet with her racquet across her throat.

"What have you been doing to my friend Val, eh?" she demanded through gritted teeth. Val was slightly taken aback by Tabitha's aggression.

Anne struggled to get free and screamed, "Get off me!"

Tabitha's response was to discard the racquet and shuffle forward until she had Anne's head locked firmly between her thighs, squeezing her head, and muffling her mouth with her crotch. Anne's eyes bulged rhythmically in an otherwise placid, pale face as her legs kicked wildly.

Val stood by, not sure whether to intervene or not. Tabitha seemed to be enjoying restraining Anne and seeing her discomfort. Tabitha looked up at him and barked an order, "Don't just stand there, Val. Find something to tie her hands and legs with." She smirked as she noticed Val's dithering and his worried frown.

"Erm... yes, there's some tape in the kitchen drawer."

"Then get it!" Tabitha commanded, for she was now in total control. Together they bound Anne's legs and arms and were about to put tape over her mouth when they noticed she was starting to fit as white foam started to appear between her lips.

"Oh, my word! She's a synth!" Tabitha said.

"Are you sure?" Val replied.

"Yes, I've seen one at work, and the foam smells oily. Here, smell it."

Val leaned in and concurred. "Oh, yes, wow! She's just so real! Now I know who she reminds me of - she's got the same jerky head movements as my AI bot at work and the virtual assistant at the dating agency!"

Tabitha stood up and put her hands on her hips. "I bet she's got realistic body parts as well, eh?"

"Oh, er, well, we never got that far..." Val stammered.

"Ha!" Tabitha laughed, "you've been had! I heard they were testing new realistic synths as companions. Now you've dated one."

"A malfunctioning one," Val added miserably.

Tabitha found the sleep mode switch under Anne's hair at the back of her head. Standing up, she looked at her handiwork with satisfaction.

"Right, she's turned off," Tabitha said as she turned to Val, her hair slightly dishevelled after the skirmish, but with a look of triumph on her wide-eyed, rosy-cheeked, adrenaline-pumped face. She laughed at him with a mocking look.

"You won't tell anyone, will you, Tabitha?" Val stammered, feeling distinctly uneasy.

"Well, Val, you dating a synth is some story."

"Please don't," he begged.

"You're starting to sound like a bit of a pathetic whiner, Val. You owe me for my silence on this. Come on, let's call your porter to help remove her."

*****

At work the next day, Val felt deeply miserable. His date had turned out to be a disturbingly realistic AI bot, and he'd seen a cruel streak in the delectable Tabitha, adding to the feeling that she'd never be a suitable partner for him. She may have been beautiful, but she was a career-obsessed high achiever with a ruthless streak. Tabitha and Bart deserved each other.

Nisha came in and he tried to snap out of it.

"Are you alright, Mr Hanwell?" she asked, with a note of concern in her sing-song voice. "Is that a slight bruise on your cheek?"

Val rubbed his face. "Oh, yeah, just a little domestic accident, nothing to worry about. What have you got for me?"

"Well, I've been through the data and identified all the errors." She showed him her tablet with an air of triumph. He quickly scrolled through the data sheets looking at the highlighted fields and sat back, smiling.

"Great job, Nisha. I'd like you to prepare a summary report for me to take to a meeting with the market research agency." She beamed with pleasure. *Why didn't the agency match me with a nice girl like her?*

"Valentine! To my office!" the harsh rasping voice of ASB cut through the walls, almost stripping the wallpaper. He got up and moved towards her glass cubicle, passing the nervous, unconvincing smile of her PA, and entered her room in a growing state of dread.

"Sit down," she ordered. He'd never been invited to sit before, nor seen her attempt a smile - it chilled him to the bone. *Where did her neck end and her head begin?* It was impossible to tell.

"I want to talk to you about the new market research data," she oozed.

Val gulped. *Has she found out there was a mistake in the data that I hadn't spotted or reported? This could spell the end...*

Through her crocodile smile she rasped, "I've had a call from the CEO, and he says that this job is suddenly top priority. He wants to see the topline summary as soon as possible. Furthermore, he's expecting me to play a part in the presentation to the board of directors, so you'll need to write me in. Valentine, it seems that we'll be working together on this one."

Val was taken aback. Not only was she not criticising him, but she'd been instructed from higher up the chain that this was a priority job. *She wants me to write her into MY presentation. In Miles's absence, I'm the only one who can do this. She knows nothing about the subject matter, so she'll be totally reliant on me!*

"Erm, Alisha," Val said, "about the warning memo you issued. We both know it's baseless and I don't want it on my record. I'd like you to withdraw it."

She dropped her smile and glared at Val, but spoke in what must have been her pleasant, conciliatory voice, "Of course, Valentine. Consider it rescinded. Now, give me a timeline so I can get back to the CEO…"

Val strode out of her office, feeling ten feet tall. The tables had turned. It was as if the weight of the world had slipped off his shoulders. He called his team to a meeting to get a status report on where they were.

"This job has attracted the attention of the CEO and the eyes of the board of directors are on us. This is now top priority."

Sally positively sparkled with enthusiasm and looked at him with a keen, fixed stare, as if he were the oracle. Dan clicked and his mouth turned up in a mimicked grin.

"But there's an error in the data that'll need to be rectified. I'm working on that with Nisha and hopefully, we'll have a new data set by late afternoon tomorrow. Then you'll have to go through it again and make the necessary adjustments. I want to see bar charts and bullet points by the end of the day. I'm going to a meeting with the research agency in the morning to discuss the glitches in the data. Until we've got the revised data set, work on the framework of the report and collate the background information for the appendices."

Val felt re-energised and called Nisha to tell her that, in the absence of her manager, she should accompany him to the meeting with the market research agency in the morning.

That evening was the dreaded Valentine's ball for the B-grade managers. Val was resigned to going alone, until a call from Tabitha changed that. Tabitha had been forced to ditch Bart as her plus-one, as, despite her father's help in getting him an interview for a promotion, he'd failed to impress, and remained a senior executive in category C, and was therefore ineligible. Valentine was duly recruited as her new date.

Tabitha looked amazing in a sequin mini dress, offset by a gleaming pearl necklace her mother had given her. They chatted about work and their promotion prospects as they waited their turn to enter the glass-domed floating restaurant and be name-checked by an AI bot who handed them champagne flutes and pointed them to the table plan.

Tabitha chatted to some familiar faces, and Val smiled and replied to questions with brief answers. There were a dozen managers that he knew, and he recognised the agency research manager that he was due to meet the following morning. He introduced himself and chatted to him whilst Tabitha mingled.

Val ordered the fillet steak, a rare luxury, and they chatted to the others sat on their table of twelve. Tabitha excused herself and left Val to his thoughts and to fiddle with the stem of his wine glass. Val's roving eye passed over the heads of his fellow diners to some pictures on the wall. One showed St Paul's Cathedral standing magnificently, taken from what had once been the Millennium Bridge, now under ten feet of water. The dome of the old cathedral still stood defiantly above the waterline.

It had been ten years since a coup by a group within the old Conservative Party had seized power and abolished elections. Val smirked at the memory. Muted outrage from the soon-banned liberal media was the only opposition to the bloodless takeover. Voter apathy had paved the way and indifference greeted the power grab as minds were focused instead on the consequences of the devastating floods. Martial law had been declared and all but the healthy, working-age Londoners had been evacuated from the sunken city. Now the final wave of evacuations was due to take place in a few weeks. London's time was up.

"And about time too," Val muttered, unaware that Tabitha had just approached their table from behind.

As she sat down, she said, "Oh, did I really take that long? I was just saying hi to a couple of friends."

Val blushed. "Oh, I didn't mean you... I was reflecting on the various waves of evacuation, if you'll forgive the pun."

Tabitha smiled, but glanced about furtively. "Well, don't reflect out loud, Val. You know it's frowned upon to talk of the past."

"Yes, there's little good in that sorrowful land," he whispered, leaning towards her.

She returned his smile and put her hand on his. "You know, I'm told by a real estate friend that working couples can apply for a house with a garden."

Val locked onto her cool, blue-eyed stare, thinking that there were worse fates. "A house would be infinitely preferable to a boxy apartment." He leaned forward with puckered lips and was duly rewarded with the lightest of pecks.

"I could join a golf club and feel the grass under my feet, for a change."

"We'll join a country club, my love, so I can keep an eye on you."

Val raised his glass and clinked it against hers in a toast. He'd unexpectedly been promoted from racquet ball partner to love interest. His future would be mapped out by the regime and his wife; he'd be a contented pawn in a rigged game. Switch off, tune in, and acquiesce. A Stepford Husband. A regime stooge with his moral filter set to "off".

"Sounds perfect. Can I take it that we're engaged, then?"

"Absolutely!" Tabitha trilled, causing heads to turn. "You post a notice in *The British Times* tomorrow and tag me. I'll get us on the housing list. Oh, this is perfect, Val! I'm so happy!"

She clapped her hands and regarded him as she might a mouse caught on a trap.

She stood and ran in tiny steps around the table, then threw her arms around his neck as he pushed his chair back to stand up. Cheers and applause ran around the room as she passionately kissed him. Val tongued and sucked, taking in the flavours of her strawberry lip gloss and the Chardonnay. His arms slipped around her slim waist, and he pulled her into him. There could be worst fates, he mused, as he came up for air. They both went their separate ways in hover taxis, as she still needed to give Bart the bad news that he was dumped.

*****

The following morning, Val chatted with Nisha in they as they skimmed over the lagoon to their meeting with the market research agency manager. When Nisha asked about the previous night's ball, he dismissed it in a couple of sentences, but mentioned that he'd met the man they were about to meet. He hadn't slept well and had woken in a sweat after a dream where he was being swallowed whole by a giant-sized Tabitha.

Nisha was smartly dressed in a trouser suit and her hair was tied up in a bun. She told him she flat shared with a friend, wasn't in a serious relationship, and had always wanted to work for a corporation that had an environmental focus. In Val's eyes, her part-Indian heritage gave her a wonderfully exotic quality that added to her mystique and serene beauty.

The meeting went well, and Val succeeded in making the agency manager squirm. He was offered profuse apologies for the error and was told it would be corrected immediately and new data sets sent over first thing in the morning; they'd work on it that night. Val left the building feeling energised and in control. He'd got his zip back.

"Let's go for a coffee," he said to Nisha, "my treat."

They crossed the road, and he guided her into a Moonbeams – there seemed to be one on every street now. "Order what you like, you deserve it," he said casually, as they sat in a circular booth. She surprised him by ordering a chocolate shake and a plant-based cheeseburger with fries. Val could only face some waffles with maple syrup with his shake.

"Wow! Okay, I know all about executives starving on low wages! Say, what are you doing on Saturday night?"

"Are you asking me out?"

"There's a new restaurant that's just opened that specialises in flavoured fungi," he said.

She turned to face him, flicking her long, black hair over her shoulder. Val was captivated by her easy, natural beauty allied to a shy, but determined nature. They could both sense an impending shift in their relationship.

"Then we'd better keep up to date with the latest culinary fashions," she purred.

They laughed as they slurped their shakes. Perhaps for the first time, when it actually mattered, he listened intently, absorbing the detail of everything she was telling him, asking pertinent questions, as an inner calm and clarity of purpose descended on him. The conversation flowed naturally, without manufactured responses on his part designed to deflect or seek an advantage. Nisha excused herself and he was left alone with his thoughts.

I need to get Tabitha out of my life. Our engagement must be nipped in the bud. I won't tolerate being bullied or being someone's plaything any longer. I can sense a sea-change in my fortunes - my Valentine's date wasn't the perfect match, after all.

*****

Shafts of sunlight through the slats of his east-facing window blinds irked Val as he struggled to wake up. The screen of his news port was beeping and the words "News Flash" ran across the screen, white on red. He rolled towards his bedside table and pressed the play button.

"Breaking news of direct consequence to Valentine Hanwell," a synthetic voice chimed.

Val sat up and watched in horror as the Port and Docks building was shown collapsing into the waters of the lagoon, causing the nearby boats to rock on its outward concentric waves.

"An estimated thirty workers are reported missing in the collapse of the Port and Docks building at Blackfriars in London Central, 7.30 am this morning," the voice recited in an emotionless tone that only served to heightened Val's sense of shock and alarm. Despite the early hour, he knew there'd be shift workers on most of the floors. There must have been around three hundred people in the building. He had long suspected such disasters underestimated the number of fatalities.

There was no answer from Sally's phone. Next, he called Nisha.

"Hi, Val," she said, her voice sending a wave of relief over him. "I'm alright. I was in early, but I managed to get out just before the collapse."

Val could see the anguish etched on her face on his tiny screen and he wanted to be with her. "I'm so relieved you're alright, Nisha. I'm coming down there now."

"Meet me at Moonbeams on the South Bank," she replied. "Once I'm checked off as safe, I'll make my way there."

Val got a hover taxi there, conscious that Tabitha hadn't called him to check if he'd been at work when the building collapsed. Perhaps she was still sleeping. He knew now that he couldn't go through with a marriage of convenience to Tabitha. He couldn't live with the regret and disappointment.

Nisha was standing outside Moonbeams, a vision of loveliness set against a backdrop of sparkling moonbeams and glowing planets. He hugged her roughly, causing her to gasp.

Nisha pushed back, her big, brown eyes welling up with tears. "Val, I'm so glad you're here, it was so terrible!" She sobbed and fell into his arms, her body shaking with emotion.

Val kissed her forehead, and she managed a tear-stained smile. "Come on, let's get a coffee and some waffles, and you can tell me what happened. I think this means our relocation to New Britannia will be speeded up."

"Yes, and the chance of a fresh start," she said, squeezing his arm. "I don't think ASB got out," she added.

"Out of despair comes warmth and light," Val quipped, then apologised on seeing her disapproving look. The fog of the lingering hangover from the ball had lifted to reveal calmness, elation, and clarity of mind.

They were guided to a booth by a bot-waiter and they placed their order. Nisha explained how she was in the ground-floor canteen when the siren sounded and was able to exit the building before the rush of those from the upper floors. As the noise of the crumbling building reached deafening proportions, a security guard had detached the float she was standing on, with about a hundred others, and they floated free of the horrific collapse, riding a wave that added to their distress.

"It was the most awful thing I've ever experienced, Val, all those people…"

"I don't know what to say, Nisha." He leaned forward and squeezed her hand. "To think, I could have been in a morning meeting on the eleventh floor. Did you see Sally? I'll try her number again."

He looked balefully at his phone as his call went to voicemail. He had no missed calls. They ate and drank in silence.

"How was the ball?" Nisha asked, looking up from her waffles.

"Oh, quite tedious, really. I was drafted in as a late replacement date by my racquetball partner, Tabitha, and found out how little I have in common with her. You know, conversing with her has made me realise that in the little time we've spent together, I much prefer your company."

"Then perhaps fate has thrown us together, Mr Hanwell."

"And maybe Cupid's wandering arrow has finally found its target," Val replied, putting an arm around her shoulder, and drawing her close to him. They shared a laugh as the bot waiter, programmed to recognise signs of romance, held out a red rose and played a tinny chorus of, "I will always love you".

They kissed and then Nisha said, "Our building collapsed and we're falling in love. A very modern romance."

"Here we are, at the death of London, plotting our escape. Someone told me that if we got engaged, we could apply for a house with a garden in the Peak District. Things are definitely looking up."

Val looked at his bleeping phone and pressed "not available" on Tabitha's face. He called over the bot waiter and paid with a tap of his ID card. With the hover taxi ordered, he turned to Nisha with a natural smile. "Let's go to mine and firm up our new age alliance."

"Can I arrange a hover taxi for you, Sir?" The bot-waiter droned.

"Erm, perhaps a gondolier would be more apt," Val replied. He smiled at Nisha who rewarded his romantic notion with a hug.

Ensconced in the motorised gondolier, replete with striped-shirted bot-pilot, they barely noticed the crash as the remnants of London Port and Docks House splashed into the green lagoon behind them. A wave soon caught them up and Nisha let out a 'wooo' as they were swept forward, giggling, towards their new life together.

Author's Note

All stories come from somewhere; the seeds of ideas planted in the author's fertile imagination sprout from lived experiences and learned sources that spark inspiration. These are mine.

Prologue – The Day our World Changed. This prologue verse imagines the sense of 'shock and awe' experienced by a native tribe when Roman soldiers first came to their village. This verse began its life as a poetic reflection on the origins of life on the banks of the river Thames before the Roman occupation. Julius Caesar's two reconnaissance missions in 55 and 54 BCE made first contact with Briton tribes in the South East, notably the *Cantii*, after whom Kent is named, the *Trinovantes* and *Catuvelauni* who inhabited the area around what is now Greater London. Caesar's mission is thought to have triggered the start of trade between Roman Gaul and Britannia, and information gathered no doubt fed into the planning of the full-scale invasion of 43 CE in the reign of Emperor Claudius.

Londinium Falling. An early version of this story was modified after reading Life in Roman London by Simon Webb. I learned some useful facts, such as the decision by General Paulinus to withdraw Londinium's garrison in advance of Boudicca's attack as the settlement lacked proper defenses and the modest-sized garrison would easily be overrun by superior numbers. However, some remained to be slaughtered, with evidence including many skulls of severed heads found in the Walbrook and washed into the Thames. I also learned that the main thoroughfare running east to west through the heart of the early city was called the *Via Decumena*, connecting two hills on which the first army camps would have been established.

Following the invasion of Britain by the Romans in 43 CE, they established a lightly guarded port on the north bank of the river Tamesis (named after a local river god, in time, becoming the Thames). But from where did the Romans take their name, Londinium? Their tactic of appeasing local tribes by adopting their place names could provide a clue. Geoffrey of Monmouth in his 1136 work, The History of the Kings of Britain, proposes that London/Londinium is named after a pre-Roman native king, King Lud. The western gate to the walled city built by the Romans (possibly on the site of a demolished iron age fort) is stilled called Ludgate, and a medieval statue to King Lud and his sons once stood there. One source gives a date of 66 BCE for the burial of King Lud under the Ludgate. He was succeeded as king of the *Trinovantes* by his son, Cassivellaunus, who opposed Julius Caesar on his second expedition in 54 BCE. Cassivellaunus is accepted as a historical figure as he is named by a Roman historian. Pre- and post-Roman history is hazy due to a lack of surviving written records.

Londinium grew into modest-sized settlement, hemmed in on three sides by a ditch, bank and perhaps a wooden stockade, by the time of the Iceni Uprising, led by Queen Boudica, in 60/61 CE. My story is from the point of view of the terrified defenders, few in number, and aware that nearby Camulodunum (Colchester) had already been burnt to the ground with all occupants slaughtered. When news of this catastrophe reached General Paulinus, he rode to Londinium with a cavalry unit, but to the inhabitant's despair, ordered the abandonment of the city following his assessment that it could not be defended. He led the garrison, followed by those willing to leave, northwards to join up with the main body of the Ninth Legion.

His tactics proved sound, as after Boudica had burnt both Londinium and Verulamium (St Albans) to the ground, the Ninth legion met them in battle and destroyed the rebel army. Boudica was thought to have committed suicide rather than be captured.

My story is a work of fiction, although the sacking and burning of Londinium by Boudica's vengeful army and slaughter of those they found there did happen. Procurator Decianus was in charge of the province's treasury and was most likely based in Londinium. As controller of the military budget, he was at odds with General Paulinus, and therefore, for the purposes of my story, I've decided that he remained with a modest guard and an escape plan, gambling on the possibility that Boudica would not attack Londinium and instead choose to move north to Verulamium. As it turned out, she attacked both settlements.

Archaeologists have discovered a 'red layer' about 13 feet below present-day street level that is a stratum of fired clay about 18 inches thick – all that remains of the first city of Londinium. The red layer is clay that once covered the walls, roofs and floors of buildings burnt by Boudica's army. This red layer has enabled archaeologists to map the outline and extent of pre-Boudican London.

Londinium – London
Camulodunum – Colchester (50 miles north-east of London)
Verulamium – St Albans (22 miles north of London)

A Summer's Disquiet is a dramatization of the real events of the Peasant's Revolt in the summer of 1381. The framework for this story of two men who are set on a bloody collision course is inspired by a truly gripping historical account by Dan Jones in his book, Summer of Blood. My story centres on the characters of rebellion leader, Wat Tyler, and his antagonist, the Lord Mayor of London, Sir William Walworth. In fact, all the main characters are historical figures, and King Richard II was 14 years old at the time, lauded by historians for his bravery in agreeing to meet with the rebellion leaders. Geoffrey Chaucer, author of The Canterbury Tales, was living in rooms above the Aldgate at the time of the revolt.

Their lives, careers and fates became intertwined as truly remarkable events were played out in June 1381. The eventual dispersal of the rebel army by King Richard and his supporters was not the end, as retribution followed as ringleaders of the uprisings were hunted down and executed in the weeks and months after the rebellion almost succeeded in toppling the monarch and seizing London. None of their demands were actioned.

As Richard's reign progressed, he became more of a tyrant, exiling or executing anyone who crossed him. Perhaps the near catastrophe of the Peasant's Revolt had made him feel insecure and fed a growing paranoia? He made the mistake of disinheriting and exiling his popular and charismatic cousin, Henry Bolingbroke, son of John of Gaunt and heir to the House of Lancaster. Henry returned to England with an army in 1399 and deposed Richard, becoming King Henry IV. Richard was not seen again and some historians believe he was imprisoned and starved to death.

Burning Shadows. The Great Fire of London started in Thomas Farriner's bakery on Pudding Lane on the night of 1st September 1666. It was speculated, in a television documentary, that the cause may have been that the oven door was left open and a spark jumped out to ignite a reed mat. The wind direction at the time was east to west, and the dry conditions allied with closely grouped and combustible houses, ensured the fire spread quickly. King Charles II didn't flee London from the encroaching fire, as William Say suggests in the story. Perhaps on the advice of courtiers, the king and his brother, the Duke of York, took the opportunity to salvage their tarnished reputations by remaining to organise firefighters and the deployment of the cavalry to pull down houses to make fire breaks. Their efforts, perhaps aided by a dying wind, succeeded in stopping the fire's spread and, on the fourth day, the Great Fire burnt out. The damage caused by the Great Fire was immense: 436 acres of London were destroyed, including 13,200 houses and 87 out of 109 churches. An accurate death toll was not recorded – the official figure was a mere six deaths.

Lawyer and Member of Parliament, William Say, was one of 59 signatories to King Charles I's execution order in 1649, and is thought to have drafted the document. He was never captured, and an entry in Wikipedia tells us he is thought to have died in 1666, but where and of what cause, remains unknown. An entry in the biography of William Say on the British Civil Wars website tells us: "He joined [General] Ludlow at Vevey in Switzerland until 1664 and is believed to have been involved in plots against the government of England in 1665-6. He probably died in the Netherlands around 1666." (www.bcw-project.org).

Many Regicides were buried in unmarked graves for fear their remains would be exhumed by vengeful Royalists (as were the bodies of Cromwell and Ireton) and their skulls displayed on spikes as traitors. The only other historical figure in the story, apart from Say, is Sheriff of London, Sir William Hooker. It is not known if William Say returned to England during his exile – I picked him for my story because of uncertainty over his fate and the likelihood that he was still alive in 1666.

Holly's Dream. Between 1609 and 1814, the surface of the river Thames froze over twenty-four times. Londoners marked some of these occasions with Frost Fairs, erecting market stalls, playing games and cooking meat on the icy surface of the river. Holly's Dream is set in 1814, the year of the last frost fair, during the reign of 'mad' King George III. It was the year before the Battle of Waterloo, where the Duke of Wellington and his allies finally put an end to Napoleon's dream of a European empire ruled by France and cemented Britain's rise as a major military power.

Cherry Blossoms Fall. In this story, all characters are fictious except Professor Keith Simpson, a pathologist during the War who gave evidence in a number of criminal cases and developed a groundbreaking method for identifying corpses using a facial recognition technique based on overlaying photographic negatives. He published a text book, Forensic

Medicine, 1947, that became the starting point for the new science of criminal pathology. A serial killer who became known the "Blackout Ripper" took advantage of the cover of darkness and murdered at least four women over a period of six days during the blackouts in London. The killer was a young airman of the RAF named Gordon Cummins. Professor Simpson gave forensic evidence at his trial.

After the German air force, the Luftwaffe, had failed to destroy the Royal Air Force in mid-1940 in advance of a planned invasion, they resorted to bombing the city of London, and other industrial cities, in a campaign of terror aimed at destroying not only infrastructure but citizen morale. From 7 October 1940 to 6 June 1941 almost 28,000 high explosive bombs and over 400 parachute mines were recorded landing on Greater London, killing over 43,500 civilians. Daylight bombing was abandoned after October 1940 as the Luftwaffe experienced unsustainable losses.

There was also a tactical switch by Hitler of military resources from Western Europe to the Eastern front at this time. The air raid by over 500 aircraft against central London on 10–11 May 1941 was a catastrophic event that led to the highest nightly casualty figure. On this one night, over 700 tons of high explosives and more than 80 tons of incendiaries were dropped. More than 2,000 fires were started that night affecting 61 London boroughs. Around 700 acres of the city were damaged by fire and more than 1,300 people were killed, over 1,600 seriously wounded and 12,000 made homeless.

The Blitz led to the largest internal migration of people in Britain's history, including the mass evacuation of over 1.5 million children, from cities and ports to rural locations. On a personal note, both of my parents experienced the Blitz. My mother, Agnes, was a schoolgirl in Liverpool during the Blitz when Liverpool's docks were heavily bombed. The family lived near the south docks in Garston. She was evacuated, with her sister Margaret, to a farm in Maghull in South Lancashire, where she had to help out with farm chores, knit scarves and jumpers beside the wireless in the evenings and do child minding. This lasted only a few months, as the girls seized the opportunity to return home at Christmas of 1940 for a break, but did not return to the Robinson farm, seeing out the war with their family in heavily bombed Garston. All the Neil family survive the war, despite a number of houses in their street being destroyed. Around 4,000 people were killed in the Liverpool Blitz.

My father, Thomas Henry Walker, was a teenager living on the outskirts of Belfast in Northern Ireland during the war. He would have witnessed the fires that raged in the aftermath of the bombings. Belfast docks were subjected to four bombing raids and resultant fires storms during the war by the Luftwaffe, killing over 1,000 and wounding around 1,500, destroying over 1,300 houses and damaging many more.

Well over 60,000 British civilians were killed across the country and many more injured in German bombing raids during the war. Many more German civilians were killed in retaliatory allied bombings before the war in Europe ended in 1945.

Brian's Beat started its life as a flash fiction story of an art gallery guard. I then had the idea of expanding this into a series of episodes in the life of a fictional policeman. It starts in the Swinging Sixties, placing Brian as a young PC at the time of the football World Cup in 1966 amidst the factual account of the trophy's theft and recovery. In 1969 the Beatles gave their last ever live performance on the roof of Apple Records in Carnaby Street in London. A friend of mine put me in touch with a man who had been the office junior at Apple Records at the time of the rooftop gig, and he gave me an insight into his job and memories of working for the band. Listening to his recollections gave me the idea for this story.

My research uncovered a news report of a real bank robbery that took place at Baker Street in 1971 that forms the background to the third story, *The Stakeout*. *The Waters of Time* and *Nelson's End* are works of fiction. I wanted to show this period of rapid technology-driven change from the 1960s to the turn of the millennium that encompassed the coming of the internet, email, wifi and mobile phones that revolutionised our lives and working practices.

I worked in London in the newspaper industry from 1985 to 1995, and transitioned from pre- to post-internet working practices in the workplace. I was the first in my marketing department to go on a desktop publishing course in 1989 and started producing in-house promotional and sales brochures. A group of us also went on personal computer training courses, and by 1992 we had moved away from Fleet Street to a new, modern building, Ludgate House, on the southern end of Blackfriars Bridge. The secretaries who had once typed our reports had been re-trained as marketing assistants. It was the start of a technological revolution in which some were left behind; but, as a younger member of the department, I was fortunate to have been one who thrived. I remember having a first-generation mobile phone, a Motorolla with a pull-up antenna, standing on a street corner waving it in the air to improve the reception and shouting into it to be heard. The range at that time was a couple of miles. It was more of a gimmick in 1991, but soon developed into the gadget we now can't live without.

The Seesaw See of Fate is a story built around my memories of working in London at that time, and draws on my notes after going on *The London Literary Pub Crawl* in Fitzrovia and Soho in 2015. Similarly, **Mac the Ripper** was written after going on a Jack the Ripper walking tour in Whitechapel around the same time.

Geraniums was written in the wake of a series of terrorist bombings in London in July 2005 that caused both fear and indignation amongst the local population. The 7th July 2005 London bombings, also referred to as 7/7 (Britain's version of 9/11), were a series of four coordinated suicide attacks carried out by Islamic terrorists in London that targeted commuters travelling on the city's public transport network during the morning rush hour.

Three individuals separately detonated homemade bombs in quick succession aboard London Underground trains across the city and, later, a fourth terrorist detonated another bomb on a double-decker bus in Tavistock Square. The train bombings occurred on the Circle line near Aldgate and at Edgware Road, and on the Piccadilly line near Russell Square.

Apart from the bombers, 52 UK residents of 18 different nationalities were killed and more than 700 were injured in the attacks, making it the UK's deadliest terrorist incident since 1988 when an onboard bomb brought down Pan Am Flight 103 near Lockerbie. (source: Wikipedia)

The London bombing explosions were caused by improvised explosive devices packed into backpacks. The bombings were followed two weeks later by a series of attempted attacks that failed to cause injury or damage. The security forces nipped many subsequent planned attacks in the bud through a hastily assembled intelligence-gathering network.

Blue Sky Thinking was inspired by a news report from 2014 that caught my eye when I was looking for short story ideas. Convicted fraudster, Neil Moore, used an illicit mobile phone to create a fake email account to send bail instructions to the prison staff.

He was released in March 2014 and his deception was only uncovered when solicitors went to interview him three days later, only to find him gone.

The prosecution at a subsequent hearing described Moore's behaviour as "ingenious" criminality. After three days of enjoying a lavish lifestyle, he gave himself up. He was quoted as saying, "The way I contrived my escape was potentially more of a threat to the integrity of the prison system, and therefore to the public, than the mere use of brute force." I have a vague memory of also reading about another prisoner who forged his early release letter, but I can't find any mention of it in an internet search. Perhaps I dreamt it. As I write this in September 2023, another prisoner has recently escaped from Wandsworth Prison, captured after four days.

I decided to build a story around this, but base it at Belsize Prison in south-east London rather than Wandsworth, so that I could indulge my desire to mention something that had fired my young imagination, namely Magwitch's escape from a prison hulk across the muddy Thames estuary marsh, from Charles Dickens' *Great Expectations*.

Valentine's Day was conceived as a vehicle to exorcise the ghost of my passing from the London corporate world to the freedom of becoming a voluntary worker in a developing country. The year was 1994 and I had recently been promoted to Marketing Manager in the group marketing department one of the UK's largest newspaper publishing groups. I enjoyed my work and this was my second promotion in eight years – providing market research and marketing support for over 100 newspaper titles.

By the mid-90s, the heady days of corporate takeovers had waned and groups were streamlining, tightening their belts and downsizing by selling off fringe assets. And so, my company decided to downsize and get rid of group functions and attendant staff in advance of a sale. They opted for penny pinching and unsentimental expediency and appointed a troubleshooting Marketing Director whose sole remit was to harass and intimidate, until we got the message we were no longer wanted and resigned. The two senior managers were the first to go, one by early retirement, the other, relocation, and I was left exposed as the last one who actually knew what we were supposed to be doing and how to organise it.

Fortunately, I had three very capable executives and we battened down the hatches to provide a fire-fighting service to our publishing centres whilst being harassed with warning memos by the unblinking bully who was our new boss. I completed a major market research project and delivered the presentations to the board's satisfaction, then resigned. Leaving on a high was cathartic, and I felt cleansed. This was quite normal in the nineties, a feature of corporate London's re-adjustment after the borrowing-to-buy spree of the late eighties had righted itself. There were many casualties at the coalface of capitalism, and I was one. My beautiful career in tatters, I re-set myself on a publishing development project in Zambia, going on to launch my own publishing and marketing business out there.

My stressful ordeal at the hands of a bullying Marketing Director is at the heart of this story. Much of the rest is pure fiction. In this much revised version of the original story, I decided to set it during the death throes of an imagined future London, flooded and planning a final evacuation to a new town on higher ground.

In April 2023, a BBC News report announced that a group of scientists who work with satellite data said the acceleration in the melting of Earth's ice sheets is unmistakable and undeniable. They calculate the planet's frozen poles lost 7,560 billion tonnes in mass between 1992 and 2022. Seven of the worst melting years have occurred in the past decade. This ice loss is five times what it was 30 years prior to the report.

NASA have been measuring rises in sea level since 1993 and recently announced that the world's sea levels are rising at an average of 0.13 inches (3.3ml) a year over a 30-year period, but this is accelerating due to warming air and sea temperatures. Coastal settlements are increasingly at risk of flooding and already some countries are taking steps to move populations inland, abandoning low lying coastal settlements. It's real. It's happening. London, after 2,000 years of history, is likely to disappear beneath the waves before the end of this century, joining an Atlantis class of submerged cities. As the rate of polar ice melt quickens, the shadow of an uncertain future hangs ominously over coastal communities.

About the Author

Tim Walker is an independent author living near Windsor in the UK.

Born in Hong Kong in the Sixties, Tim grew up in Liverpool where he began his working life as a trainee reporter on a local newspaper. He went on to attain an honours degree in Communication Studies in South Wales before moving to London where he worked in the newspaper publishing industry for ten years.

In the mid-90s he opted to spend a few years doing voluntary work in Zambia through VSO, running an educational book publishing development programme. After this, he set up his own marketing and publishing company in Lusaka, Zambia's capital. He returned to the UK in 2009.

His creative writing journey began in earnest in 2014, as a therapeutic activity whilst recovering from cancer treatment. In addition to short stories, he researched and wrote a five-book history-meets-legend fiction series, *A Light in the Dark Ages*.

More recently, he has written a dual timeline historical novel set at Hadrian's Wall, *Guardians at the Wall*. Somewhere along the way, he also wrote a three-book children's series with his daughter, Cathy, *The Adventures of Charly Holmes*.

Find Tim Walker's author pages on Amazon and Goodreads, and follow him on X, formerly Twitter, and Instagram as timwalker1666.

Thank you for reading London Tales. Please leave a star rating and review on Amazon and/or Goodreads so others can benefit from your experience.

Please visit Tim's website for book news:
www.timwalker1666.wixsite.com/website

Thames Valley Tales

If you enjoyed reading *London Tales*, then why not try its companion volume, *Thames Valley Tales*?

Thames Valley Tales is a light-hearted yet thought-provoking collection of twelve stories by Tim Walker (nine in the audiobook). These tales are based on the author's experience of living in Thames Valley towns, and combine contemporary themes with the rich history and legends associated with an area stretching from the heart of rural England to London.

The collection includes *The Goldfish Bowl*, in which an unlikely friendship is struck between a pop star and an arms dealer in Goring-on-Thames; *Maidenhead Thicket*, where the ghost of legendary highwayman, Dick Turpin surprises a Council surveyor; *The White Horse* intrigue surrounding the dating of the famous chalk carving on the Berkshire Downs; *Murder at Henley Regatta*, a beguiling whodunit, and *The Colnbrook Caper*, a pacey crime thriller. *Thames Valley Tales* starts with *The Grey Lady*, a ghost story from the English Civil War, and features *The Merry Women of Windsor* in a whimsical updating of Shakespeare's classic play. The *Author's Note* explains the context and reasoning behind each story.

Thames Valley Tales oscillates from light-hearted to dark historical and at times humorous stories ideally suited to bedtime or holiday reading that will amuse, delight and, hopefully, inform the reader about the rich history of the Thames Valley as it winds 215 miles from the Gloucestershire countryside, past many towns and villages to London and out to the North Sea. The book also has a factual chapter and map of the Thames Valley showing the towns through which the 184-mile Thames Path passes. It's a walk-through history and the natural beauty of England that will inspire and captivate.

Thames Valley Tales, second edition, is available in audiobook, Kindle e-book and paperback from Amazon worldwide, and can also be found on Kindle Unlimited.

Thames Valley Tales

a collection of short stories

by Tim Walker

Printed in Great Britain
by Amazon